STEVE HIGGS
MAJESTIC MYSTERY

BOOKS

Vinci Books

vinci-books.com

Published by Vinci Books Ltd in 2026

1

Copyright © Steve Higgs 2023

The author has asserted their moral right to be identified as the author of this work in accordance with the Copyright, Designs and Patents Act 1988. This work is a work of fiction. Names, characters, places and Incidents are the product of the author's imagination or are used fictitiously. Any resemblance to actual persons, living or dead, places and incidents is entirely coincidental.

All rights reserved. No part of this publication may be copied, reproduced, distributed, stored in any retrieval system, or transmitted in any form or by any means, including photocopying, recording, or other electronic or mechanical methods, nor used as a source for any form of machine learning including AI datasets, without the prior written permission of the publisher.

The publisher and the author have made every effort to obtain permissions for any third party material used in this book and to comply with copyright law. Any queries in this respect should be brought to the attention of the publisher and any omissions will be corrected in future editions.

A CIP catalogue record for this book is available from the British Library.

Paperback ISBN: 9781036709723

The EU GPSR authorised representative is Logos Europe, 9 rue Nicolas Poussion, 17000 La Rochelle, France contact@logoseurope.eu

By Steve Higgs

Albert Smith's Culinary Capers

Pork Pie Pandemonium
Bakewell Tart Bludgeoning
Stilton Slaughter
Bedfordshire Clanger Calamity
Death of a Yorkshire Pudding
Cumberland Sausage Shocker
Arbroath Smokie Slaying
Dundee Cake Deception
Lancashire Hotpot Peril
Blackpool Rock Bloodshed
Kent Coast Oyster Obliteration
Eton Mess Massacre
Cornish Pasty Conspiracy
The Gastrothief
Lyme Regis Layover
Majestic Mystery

Blue Moon Investigations

Paranormal Nonsense
The Phantom of Barker Mill

Amanda Harper Paranormal Detective
The Klowns of Kent
Dead Pirates of Cawsand
In the Doodoo with Voodoo
The Witches of East Malling
Crop Circles, Cows and Crazy Aliens
Whispers in the Rigging
Paws of the Yeti
Under a Blue Moon
Night Work
Lord Hale's Monster
Herne Bay Howlers
Undead Incorporated
The Ghoul of Christmas Past
The Sandman
Jailhouse Golem
Sparks in the Darkness
Shadow in the Mine
Ghost Writer
Monsters Everywhere
Modern Fairy Tale
No Such Thing as Magic

Majestic Mystery

Getting Ready

"Rex, I feel like a right wally in this get up."

Rex tilted his head to one side, trying to decipher his human's words.

Unable to make sense of the old man's latest dilemma, he opted to remark, "If you want my opinion on your choice of removable pelt for today, then I would have to say that it looks a tad impractical."

Albert twitched his eyes down and left, catching sight of his dog as Rex sauntered from the room.

Over his shoulder Rex said, "It also makes you look like a bit of a wally."

Albert stared at his reflection in the mirror, grumpily fiddling with his bow tie which was perfect fifteen minutes ago when he first tied it and was still perfect now. Bedecked in a full morning suit with tails, a grey waistcoat, and a top hat, he was due to be collected in less than half an hour and was giving serious consideration to feigning that his hip had gone out and he couldn't walk. Or possibly just throwing himself down the stairs for real.

That would get him out of it.

Out of a trip to the palace to be knighted by the king.

Knight Commander of the British Empire. He'd never even heard of it until he got the letter from the palace. How could it be that Albert Smith, a former copper and son of a greengrocer was about to be granted the title of Lord and be recognised in the King's birthday honours list?

It was a rhetorical question, obviously. Albert knew precisely why he was being honoured. He saved a bunch of people and then gave away millions of pounds he'd unwittingly won. Gave it away before he even saw it. That was probably for the best, but how was he to know the attention his charitable act would attract?

There were times when he wished he'd kept it. Then he could have funded his disappearance. Not that he was short of money. His pension from a senior position in the police provided more money each month than he needed, and he'd been prudent over the years, investing and saving so Albert suspected he would run out of life before he ran out of cash.

"Are you ready, Dad?" his daughter, Selina, called up the stairs.

Left by her brothers to make sure he was ready on time, Randall and Gary were at the pub just along the road. Selina cursed them, but she'd lost the game of rock, paper, scissors used to determine who dealt with their father.

Grumbling, Albert pulled a face at his reflection and left his bedroom.

"I'm coming," he called down the stairs, using the banister for support as he descended. Going up wasn't so hard, but at nearly eighty, his legs were less inclined to descend.

Rex trotted past him, the stairs offering no such obstacle

for his young body. At the bottom, Rex turned, wagging his tail slowly as he watched the old man and waited for him to catch up.

Selina called for her daughter, Apple-Blossom, to come. The seven-year-old was lost in a world only a person her age could understand, her eyes glued to the tablet fixed between her hands.

"Apple-Blossom!" Selina raised her voice when she got no response the first time.

Jolted into action, the small voice of a girl who knew better than to sound annoyed when she said, "Coming, mummy. Sorry, I didn't hear you."

Selina ground her teeth and let it pass. Her youngest was becoming a little too precocious in recent weeks, testing her boundaries as all children do.

Selina smiled at the sight of her father. "Dad, you look wonderful. Very statesmanlike." Like her brothers, and everyone else in the family, she could not be more proud to be related to the old man about to be honoured by the king. Her father had single-handedly tracked down and brought to justice a lunatic distant relative of the reigning monarch. Earl Hubert Bacon kidnapped dozens of people and had them stashed inside an inescapable underground lair in Wales.

Selina's father, with the police after him because they believed Albert was the one behind many of the crimes that occurred during his unsanctioned investigation, tracked the Earl's agents – a team of hired mercenaries responsible for dozens of deaths – and was able to overcome them through an incredible network of friends he attracted along the way.

The tale was simply too fanciful to be true and yet it was. Then her father discovered he'd won millions on a longshot bet he'd placed almost by accident while trying to solve a murder in Melton Mowbray. Most people would take the money and look forward to a well-funded retirement, but Albert Smith gave it all away by publicly creating a charity to support those persons affected by Earl Bacon's crimes.

In the wake of the news coverage, those people and their food industry businesses were enjoying a boom in sales. There's nothing like free publicity they say, and there was a lot of it going around.

Every last one of them had sent Albert a care package of food or drink, but the term package fails to describe the magnitude of gratitude the rescued persons chose to show in gastronomic form. Trucks and vans started arriving at Albert's little semi-detached house the day after he got home. Initially he'd tried to turn the food away, but that proved futile.

Next, Albert distributed it among his friends and family, but when the gifts just kept coming, he contacted a few local homeless shelters and soup kitchens. To the best of Selina's knowledge, they were still working their way through it three months later.

"I look like a penguin," Albert grumbled at his daughter, omitting the mild expletive before it left his mouth in deference to his granddaughter's presence. Focusing on her, he said, "Apple-Blossom, you have to be the most beautiful granddaughter ever to walk the face of the earth."

"Granddad you're so silly," she giggled. Her smile ended when she remembered a question she wanted to ask. "What is Rex going to wear?"

Rex's eyebrows tried to shoot off the top of his head. "Wear? I'm a dog. I come fully clothed with a coat that stays on me. It's you weird, bald humans who need the removable ones."

Albert spotted the look on his dog's face and with a devilish grin, whipped a bow tie from a trouser pocket.

"I thought he might look good in this," Albert pumped his eyebrows at Rex.

Rex uttered something rude and made a break for it.

Selina frowned. "Wait, did he just understand what was being said?"

Albert shook his head. "Of course not, he's a dog. He must have picked up on the cues from what we were doing and because I looked his way."

The truth of the matter was that Albert knew his dog understood a great deal more than any other dog he'd ever met or heard about. Rex had an uncanny way of knowing what to do. It was how they managed to survive their journey around the British Isles. Rex came to Albert's rescue more times than he cared to mention and over the course of the months they were on the road, Albert found he could not avoid one rather worrying conclusion: that Rex was also trying to solve the cases they came across.

Watching his dog scramble around the corner and vanish from sight, Albert chuckled to himself and called out, "The back door is locked, Rex."

When he arrived in the kitchen with his granddaughter leading the way and Selina just behind, Albert found Rex staring dejectedly at the back door. Rex had figured out how to operate the handle and for that reason Albert had taken to locking it.

Five minutes later, the party arrived at the pub down the road where Albert's eldest, Gary, and his youngest, Randall, had a pint waiting for their father. There was also a gin and tonic for Selina, a fruit drink and some crisps for Apple-Blossom, and a half pint of Guinness for Rex.

Rex finished first.

"Can't dawdle, the car will be here soon," remarked Gary, checking his watch.

Albert wanted to complain that he didn't have enough time to finish his drink, but he knew that was down to how long he spent arguing with himself about his outfit.

It was expected, you see. The people from the palace were very specific about it. Quite why the king couldn't have got it over with during Albert's previous visit he had no idea. Of course, the first visit to the palace had been all business. The king wanted to thank Albert in person and discuss with him the charity he set up to help Earl Bacon's victims get back on their feet.

The palace offered to not only take on running the charity, which Albert had no desire to manage himself, but also to double the pot of money Albert pledged when the bookies handed him the cheque.

Albert was still grumbling about all the unnecessary pomp and ceremony eighteen minutes later when they loaded him into the sleek, black limousine outside the pub.

It was time to head to London and Albert's children, at least, were full of smiles. Had they known then what was going to happen that day, they might have chosen to stay in the pub.

Familiar Scent

For most people, a visit to Buckingham Palace is a big deal. That was certainly the case for Albert's three children and his granddaughter, Apple-Blossom, who could not wait to get to school on Monday to tell all her friends and show them the pictures.

Albert had other grandchildren, of course, and his two eldest children both had spouses, but the invitation was limited to four guests, so the rest were going to have to hear about it second-hand.

The limousine, hired by the palace, waltzed through the security checkpoint at the end of The Mall and pulled up to a drop off point behind another car that looked to be the twin of the one they were in.

It was a slick operation, each car deploying its passengers before gliding forward again to make room for the next. Opening the car doors were palace staff, dressed in red tunics with gold brocade that made them look like something from Downton Abbey or Cinderella, and a few steps beyond them, police with automatic weapons loitered, eyes open and alert.

Albert accepted a hand from Gary in sliding out of the car and stepping away, he straightened his jacket. He was done moaning. His kids were excited, and he recognised this was an honour. Also, he'd played what he thought would be a trump card in insisting that Rex had to be honoured too and they agreed. They were supposed to say no and that would be the end of it, but apparently the king or someone in the palace's PR department more likely, thought it was a great idea.

Whatever the case, Albert accepted there was no getting out of it. He was about to be knighted and Rex was going to be at his side when it happened.

Rex, unhappy about the bowtie around his neck and hoping there wouldn't be any other dogs around to see it was most disappointed to find two German Shepherds with the human police officer handlers looking his way.

One nudged the other and said something Rex wasn't able to hear.

Annoyed, Rex turned his head away and sniffed.

Albert, holding Rex's lead, was just starting to move forward, but found his left arm jerked backward when Rex chose not to follow.

"Rex, come on, boy," Albert encouraged.

Rex's eyes were closed. He found it helped to focus his most powerful sense if he could shut out the messages coming from the rest of them. There was a scent on the air, he'd caught it the moment he drew air into his nose. Now he needed a moment to be certain he wasn't being misled.

"Rex!" Albert hissed. Turning to Gary, he said, "I might need a hand here."

Rex tried again, but the elusive smell was gone. Opening his eyes, Rex looked at his human.

"I think he's here," Rex attempted to explain.

Albert couldn't understand and was too busy attempting to obey the request to 'move along, please, sir,' as there was a long line of cars, and his party was holding things up.

Rex trotted forward, determined to find the source of the scent if he could. It was coming from somewhere, that much he knew for sure. All he needed was a decent whiff and he would be able to track it.

Following the procession of people ahead, Albert's family found themselves entering a glamorous room. It was filled with excited babble, as the guests milling around inside were plied with glasses of champagne and offered tiny morsels of food from silver trays being carried by more of the immaculate palace staff. They were barely in the room when Randall whipped a glass of champagne from a tray that came by.

The server stopped so Gary and Selina could take one each and crouched so Apple-Blossom could have one of the 'safe-for-children' non-alcoholic drinks. Her eyes sparkled at the fizzy concoction served in an elegant champagne glass.

"Be careful with that, sweetie," warned her mother, spoiling the moment.

"I'm not going to drop it, mummy," the little girl all but growled.

Albert didn't want a drink. What he wanted was to drain off the pint of beer he regrettably chose to swiftly down before they left the pub. His bladder control still worked just fine, but that was no good reason to challenge himself. It was an hour before they would begin to be called down to meet the king and he wanted to be comfortable for the big event.

Handing Rex to Randall, he should have noticed how distracted his dog was acting, but didn't; his eyes were too busy scoping the area for a sign that might tell him which way to go for restrooms. There wasn't one, but a tell-tale line of men and women coming back and forth from one corner of the room suggested he might find what he wanted over there.

Sure enough the corner hid a narrow corridor – narrow for the palace that is – that led to what could only be described as the nicest toilets Albert had ever visited.

Coming back out two minutes later, he was heading back to the reception room when one of the palace service staff went by ahead of him. The man passed through a door and vanished from sight, but just like Rex when he caught a scent he knew, Albert was now rooted to the spot.

"Can't be," he mumbled, unable to believe his eyes.

Disorientated

Rushing forward to catch the door before it closed, Albert's fingers got pinched, but he was able to slip through a moment later, sucking on his bruised digits as he hurried to see where the man went.

Straining to remember his name, only the first part came – Cody. Cody ... something. Williams! Albert's brain supplied a last name.

"Cody Williams," Albert breathed the name as he hurried along the corridor. He last saw him in the Cornish seaside village of Looe when he ran off into the darkness following a shootout that almost got them both killed.

The man was an anti-royalist with a plan to poison a bunch of people at the engagement reception for Prince Marcus and his fiancée. Albert scuppered that plan more by accident than design, but Cody's presence here in the palace couldn't mean anything good.

It bothered Albert that he'd never thought to find out if the police ever caught him. When Albert fled Looe – the police were mistakenly after him - he left behind a brother and sister who were going to expose the conspiracy Albert disturbed. Cody's plan to kill members of the royal family might have failed, but he was guilty of murder, nevertheless. He killed one of his co-conspirators the night Albert arrived, leaving his body to be found on the beach as though he'd drowned while taking an early morning dip.

Making his way along the behind-the-scenes corridor and conscious he was in an area he wasn't supposed to be, Albert knew he ought to be creeping. That wasn't his style though. If anything, he was too old to be sneaky – sneaking required speed and agility, two attributes for which he scored low these days.

"Excuse me, sir," said a polite voice belonging to a young woman. She'd just come through the door behind Albert. "Are you looking for the restrooms?"

Albert wasn't one hundred percent certain it was Cody he saw, but the fleeting half second the man was passing across Albert's field of vision was enough to make Albert believe he needed to find out. A more cautious person might bluff, and act as though lost. If he did that, the woman would return him to the reception room and that would be that. But what if he was right?

Albert chose honesty.

"I just saw a man come in here." Albert continued in the direction he'd been walking.

"You're not supposed to be back here, sir."

"I think he's someone dangerous."

"Please come back to the reception room with me."

"If I'm right, then he's up to no good."

"Sir, I'll have to call security."

Her last statement made Albert spin around to face her. The woman, for she was a woman and not a girl, as Albert's ageing brain wanted to label her, had light brown hair and deep blue eyes. She wore the same palace livery as all the other staff and was both tall and a little skinny. She looked nervous about the prospect of raising the alarm, but also gave the impression she was about to do it.

Albert backtracked two steps.

"Do it."

"Excuse me?"

"Do it. Call security. Get the police, in fact. I think you have an anti-royalist terrorist in the palace and if I am right the police might need to evacuate the whole building."

The young woman's face showed the shock she felt upon hearing Albert's unexpected declaration.

"Oh, my goodness!" she gasped.

"Go," Albert indicated back towards the reception room on the other side of the door. "Get help."

"What's going on, Sarah?" asked a new voice.

Albert turned to find a man approaching. He was barely older than the woman, but had a capable, confident look that Sarah did not possess.

Sarah blurted, "This man says there's a terrorist here."

Speaking as though she hadn't said a word, the man pointed back to the exit.

"I'm sorry, sir. This area is reserved for palace staff only. You'll need to rejoin your party in the reception room."

"Didn't you just hear what she said?" Albert frowned.

"He wants us to call security, Chase," Sarah explained.

Chase smiled, amused by the old man's antics.

"Yes. Let's get you back to your family, shall we?" he spoke at Albert, not to him, raising his voice and talking slowly as though dealing with an idiot.

When he tried to take Albert's arm, intending to steer him in the right direction, he found the limb snapped out of his reach.

"Young man, I need you to listen …"

"What's going on?" asked another voice, this one belonging to another man. He was carrying a tray of hors d'oeuvres.

"Nothing you need to concern yourself with, Charlie," replied Chase in a dismissive tone. "This gentleman is just a little disorientated, that's all."

Albert was about ready to offer to disorientate Chase's nose when Charlie came to his rescue.

"But that's Albert Smith, you nitwit. I just heard Sarah say something about a terrorist. If Albert Smith thinks there's a terrorist here, then we have a big problem."

Charlie's concern was enough to give Chase pause and that was all it took for Charlie to seize the initiative.

He ran back to where he came from – a door on the left that led to a kitchen, Albert guessed. Moments later more people appeared, flooding into the corridor where Albert waited with Sarah and Chase.

Faces were flustered, Charlie having hyped the drama to make it sound like the palace was about to explode.

Among the new arrivals, a member of the palace security team. She was jabbering urgently into a radio and jogging in her low heels to close the distance. Dressed in a smart, but not expensive suit, Albert guessed the woman to be a police detective and was proven right when she introduced herself.

"I'm Detective Inspector Cassie Monroe, Mr Smith. I am led to believe you saw someone carrying a bomb."

"Monroe, report!" barked a voice over the radio.

She lifted it to her mouth in a snapping motion, her eyes never leaving Albert's.

"Stand by."

With a glance at Charlie who blushed deep violet in an

involuntary act of admission, Albert used a calm voice to say, "That is not what I said. I saw a man who I believe to be a staunch anti-royalist wearing palace livery. He is wanted for murder and was involved in a plot to poison guests at the engagement party of Prince Marcus and Miss Morley. I said nothing about a bomb."

Moving the radio back to her mouth, DI Munroe pressed the send button.

"Stand down. I repeat: stand down. Do not evacuate the palace. The bomb warning was an error, over."

"An error?" repeated the voice at the other end, the man's tone incredulous.

"I'm investigating now," DI Munroe advised. "I need two units to my location at the reception kitchen, over."

"I expect a full report, Munroe," barked the voice. "Two units coming your way now."

Lowering her radio, yet keeping it in her right hand, DI Munroe looked up at Albert Smith.

"Now then, sir. How about if you start at the beginning?"

Hors d'oeuvres

"Where do you think dad got to?" asked Selina looking at her watch.

"Mummy, I'm bored," said Apple-Blossom, who was also getting hungry and didn't like any of the stupid hors d'oeuvres. They all had mucky stuff on them, and they were cold. What kind of party was this if they didn't know to serve Jaffa Cakes?

Ignoring her child as she became increasingly concerned about her missing father, Selina poked Gary in the ribs.

He made an 'oof' noise and twisted to see what his sister wanted. Gary had been forced to endure many years of getting beaten up by his sister when they were young. 'She's younger than you and she's smaller,' still rang in his ears even now. Back then, Selina took full advantage of the fact that her older brother would never be believed if he claimed she was hurting him.

Now she was at it again and he still wasn't in a position to complain because he not only outranked her – all three of Albert's children were senior police detectives, but the height/size difference as children had multiplied in adulthood. He had to be twice her weight now.

"What is it?" he demanded, irritably.

Narrowing her eyes, Selina said, "Well, for one, you're married, so stop eyeing every piece of cleavage going past. Secondly, you need to go and check on dad. He's been gone too long."

Gary felt aggrieved at her accusation. Okay, so he might have happened to just accidentally notice that one or two of the ladies attending today had chosen to wear rather low-cut dresses and were sporting the kind of weapons men found impossible to resist noticing, but he was a man for goodness sake. It wasn't like he was going to go over and try chatting them up. That's what Randall was doing.

Sensing the futility in claiming his innocence, especially since he was guilty, Gary said, "How long's he been gone?"

"Too long," Selina repeated her assessment.

While above him the humans bickered, Rex looked about for food. The canapes smelled ... well, good enough to eat, and he thought it unreasonable that the trays kept going by without any coming down to his level.

His human would have snuck him a few, Rex felt confident of that, but the old man was strangely absent. There were crumbs on the floor, but nothing big enough to bother with. However, when the crowd shifted slightly, Rex spotted a low table where half a dozen or more of the little snacks had been placed. Someone was hoarding, which was fine by Rex. They wouldn't need them all and were unlikely to miss the ones he planned to take.

Unfortunately, he was still tethered to Randall, his human's youngest pup, and couldn't see a way to get free without causing a commotion.

Help came from an unexpected source.

Apple-Blossom, thoroughly bored with the day – they were going to the palace, so where were all the princesses? She had planned to spend the day riding horses and falling in love with one of the princes. She was in a palace, there had to be princes. Seven was the perfect age to be swept off her feet so far as Apple Blossom was concerned and she had spent the last two weeks trying out different ways to write Princess Apple-Blossom.

Unable to get her mother's attention, she took matters into her own hands.

Rex felt the tiny fingers fiddling with the clip for his collar, and tried to turn his head.

"Stay still, Rex," urged the little girl, whispering and not daring to check if her mother was paying her any attention.

Unexpectedly free of his tether, Rex stepped away, but then turned, unsure what he was supposed to do. 'Eat the snacks,' echoed in his head, and he was going to do precisely that, but what about the little girl?

"Go,' she urged insistently, adding a shooing gesture when Rex failed to move. Apple-Blossom liked her grand-dad's dog. He was big and friendly and had a fluffy fur coat that made him great for cuddling. She had an early memory of when Rex first came to live with her granddad, and she got to run around his garden throwing a ball for Rex to chase. That made her tired and she got to use Rex's belly as a pillow for her head while he slept and she read a book.

Believing there had to be some Jaffa Cakes somewhere, she shooed Rex until he started moving, and with a glance to check mum wasn't looking her way, she followed.

Rex cleared the table of canapes and was gone before the human who'd placed them there reached down to select one. Mission accomplished, he thought perhaps he would search for his human. The old man had been gone for a while now and Rex didn't like it. Not because he fretted when separated, but because the old man had a habit of getting himself into trouble.

However, in the moment that his paws began to move, the scent he caught a faint whiff of outside returned. This time it came with direction.

Rex gave himself a moment to confirm he wasn't wrong – his nose had never let him down before – and he set off.

Bites Owed

Securely away from her mother, Apple-Blossom wasn't sure where to go. The room was full of people, but she could see all around and there was no table laid out with child friendly treats as she very much hoped there would be.

Disappointed, she considered returning before her mother noted her absence, but when she looked, Apple-Blossom discovered she couldn't see her parent. Telling herself not to panic, even as the extreme emotion raised its ugly head, she spotted Rex going by on the other side of the room. He was heading back the way they had come in, and curious, she decided to follow.

When she had arrived in the big, posh car, Apple-Blossom had spotted gardens to the rear of the palace – they'd looked much more interesting and maybe there would be a playground where she could run around. Having Rex in tow gave her the perfect excuse too.

A few yards away, Selina was bored arguing with her brothers. Randall had cartoon love hearts where his eyes used to be. In the company of a woman made famous for winning multiple gold medals for her gymnastic prowess, he was flirting openly and not getting instantly rejected for once. Selina was happy to let him get on with it and might even have wished him luck were she not so preoccupied with where her father had gotten to.

Gary believed their father would return if left to do so, and insisted there was no need to chase him out of the gents' facilities. He would come back when he was ready.

Selina refused to settle for that plan, so was going to the gents herself. It wasn't going to be the first time she'd marched into the gentlemen's facilities. First time at the palace perhaps, and on the previous occasions she was either fetching one of her sons or acting in her official capacity as a police officer.

"Look, I'm going," she snapped at Gary, ending the argument. "Do something useful and take care of your niece for a few seconds."

Gary had a snarky retort lined up, but frowning instead, he asked, "Where is she?"

Now some distance away, Apple-Blossom was with Rex, the dog not seeing any reason to question the little girl's decision to accompany him. Besides, he had a scent in his nose, and it was someone he needed to bite.

Someone he owed a bite.

Names had little meaning to Rex, and he had no idea what the human whose scent he now tracked was called. It was of no consequence. If he could follow the smell to its source, he would give chase and wait for his human or the police to arrive. What Rex did know was where he first encountered the scent. It was in Cornwall where he and his human found themselves involved in yet another fun adventure.

It was where he almost caught Tanya, a woman who

very definitely deserved to get bitten. There were seals, and boats and a dead body he found on the beach. The scent he now followed belonged to the man at the centre of all that drama and Rex wanted to find him.

The scent, however, proved elusive. It didn't help that they were inside a building with so many other people. The odour each human carried intertwined and overlapped with all the others. If his target had touched an object along the way, it would give Rex a waypoint to check the smell and move on, but the man's scent was in the air and nowhere else. Furthermore, it was everywhere or, at least, it lingered enough places that Rex could tell the man he tracked wasn't a new arrival.

Like going into a person's home, the scent of that person is everywhere. Sure, you can track it to find their exact location, but that's in a standard sized domicile, not a palace arranged over multiple floors with more rooms than an average street.

Ten minutes into his search, Rex acknowledged, with some irritation, that he wasn't going to be able to track his target. The scents overlapped constantly where the man had gone back and forth multiple times. It was one of those occasions when his sense of smell had to take a back seat.

He was going to have to use his eyes instead.

It was when he looked up and paid attention to what he could see that things changed that day.

Missing Person Report

"I'm telling you; I know what I saw," Albert insisted. Encouraged to explain who he thought they needed to find, Albert provided a name and a description.

Cody Williams was not listed as an employee at the palace and DI Munroe insisted their security was too tight for a person to just wander in from the street, don a uniform, and access restricted parts of the palace. Yes, something like that had happened in the past, but that was more than thirty years ago, and it only happened the once.

Diligent enough to not dismiss Albert Smith's claim out of hand when the name failed to appear in her directory of staff, DI Munroe asked if any of the other servers working today knew a man called Cody.

"He would have a Cornish accent," Albert pointed out.

"Oh, yeah?" said Chase, still unhappy that Charlie made him look bad in front of Sarah. "What does that sound like then?"

DI Munroe shot the unhelpful server a look that shut his mouth.

Addressing the group, she said, "If anyone else has pointless comments to make, I suggest they keep them to themselves. I want you all to be extra vigilant today. If you see a new member of palace staff and you are not sure who they are, challenge them. Or call for me or any member of the palace security team. Is that understood?"

She got a round of confirmations. No one knew a person called Cody, which threw Albert's claim to have seen the man even further into doubt. DI Munroe was armed with an electronic tablet on which she could access police files. Cody Williams was indeed wanted in connection with events that occurred a few months ago in Cornwall, but it didn't say he was considered likely to be pursuing a vendetta against the royal family.

"How sure are you?" DI Munroe pressed Albert. It was the third time she'd asked.

"Just as sure as last time you asked," he replied. "Look, I know better than to waste anyone's time. I think it was him. I caught the side of his face as he went through a door, as I already explained. I accept that I could be wrong, but I would be more wrong to keep quiet when I know who he is and what he is capable of."

DI Cassie Munroe couldn't argue with the old man, but harboured a worrying suspicion that Albert Smith had enjoyed the spotlight a little too much and was trying now to grab a little more before it faded completely.

Unfortunately, like the old man said, the only wrong thing to do would be to ignore the possibility that he was right.

DI Munroe's radio crackled, a short burst of static preceding a voice.

"All units, all units, please be aware there is a child missing inside the palace." The voice was male and spoke in a calm tone – this was an issue to be raised but not one the speaker felt the need to start a stampede over. "The child is a girl. Seven years old and is dressed in a pink, chiffon dress. She has blonde hair and answers to the name ..."

"Apple-Blossom," finished Albert, talking over the man on the radio.

DI Munroe jinked her eyes across to look at Albert.

"My granddaughter," he explained. Licking his lips, he added, "Look, I don't want to start a panic, but if I saw Cody Williams then he might just as easily have seen me first. He knows who I am because I almost caught him in Cornwall. If he saw me arrive with my family ..."

DI Munroe was already on it, relaying Albert's concerns back over the airwaves just as the two units she requested came through the door to join her in the kitchen.

Albert sucked in a deep breath to steady himself. He needed Rex. Rex would find his granddaughter.

Where There's Smoke

Rex peered around the corner.

"Shhhh!" hissed Apple-Blossom, her head right next to his ear so her breath tickled the fine hairs inside to make it twitch.

The twitching ear in turn tickled the tip of Apple-Blossom's nose to make her giggle and almost sneeze.

"Shhh!" she sniggered, holding Rex's ear this time to keep it still. Focussing again, she whispered, "What is she doing?"

Rex's search for Cody Williams, not that he knew the man's name, had paused when Apple-Blossom abruptly grabbed his collar. The reception room was far behind them, and they'd had to duck under a sign that read 'Restricted Area Staff Only'. Well, Apple-Blossom had to duck under it and the elegant rope from which it dangled, Rex merely walked underneath it.

Apple-Blossom read the sign and knew what it meant, but Rex wanted to go that way and maybe it would lead to the gardens. Besides, once they snuck out of the reception room where all the people were gathered, they found they could go where they chose because the rest of the palace was completely devoid of life.

Until now.

Coming around a corner, there was a woman ahead of them. Apple-Blossom's decision to stay out of sight was automatic – she was having too much fun snooping where she knew she ought not to be to get caught now. However, having ducked back out of sight to see if the woman would move on, she knew she was watching a person up to no good.

Maybe it was the generations of police officers in her family tree, or maybe it was too much time watching the way her mother observed the world; regardless, the seven-year-old intrinsically knew she was seeing a person acting furtively and that made her want to watch.

"I think ... I think she's starting a fire," Apple-Blossom murmured, mostly to herself.

The woman was much bigger than her mother. Apple-Blossom knew better than to use the word 'fat' because that was an unpleasant and negative term; they talked about such things in school. However, after noting her long, straight, dark brown hair, her deep green dress that fell almost to the floor and the matching bolero jacket employed to keep her bare shoulders warm even though it wasn't cold (also suspicious), Apple-Blossom's second grade vocabulary struggled to find a nicer word.

"Big-boned!" she snapped her fingers in excitement and had to duck again when the woman looked around to see if there was anyone there.

With the little girl holding him around his neck, Rex resisted surging forward when the woman hurried away, but the moment she turned a corner and vanished from sight, both dog and girl raced to see what she had been doing.

Rex's police dog training included exposure to fire, but understanding what it was and knowing he could rush through small amounts of it without getting burned did nothing to help in this situation. Flames and white smoke were coming from a gap between wooden panels. Scrunched up pieces of paper and a mix of twigs and straw were catching fast, yellow flames dancing before his eyes.

Backing away in fear, he bumped into Apple-Blossom who was going the other way.

Before Rex's eyes, the little girl used a slender arm to knock the mix of combustible materials out of the cubby hole into which they had been stuffed. It hit the floor, the flames growing as the mess of burning paper and straw spread out.

Rex backed away another step but this time it was to give Apple-Blossom space. Ability to stamp out fires probably wasn't an attribute the manufacturer considered when designing the shiny pink shoes on her feet, but they did the trick, nevertheless.

She used both feet, jumping about from smouldering ember to smouldering ember until they were nothing but charred ash.

Breathing a sigh of relief, she fixed her gaze on Rex.

"Dog, I think we need to follow her. She's up to no good and there's no time to fetch any grown-ups to help."

Rex came forward, delivering a quick lick to her chin. "You know something, little girl? I think that's the best idea I've heard in weeks."

They hustled, Rex trotting at a steady lope with Apple-Blossom jogging by his side.

"Wait," she begged after a few paces. "Wait, I need to take these shoes off. They are making too much noise."

Rex's paws made no noise at all, but away from the reception area the corridors were not carpeted, and the shoes Apple-Blossom wore clicked and clonked to announce their approach. Yet again Rex was impressed at the little girl's mindfulness.

It took them more than a minute to catch up with the woman who was also hurrying through the palace. They kept a safe distance behind her, tracking her through the maze of passages with ease because she still wore her shoes.

Until they lost her, that is.

Keeping a corner between them at all times so she could not spin around and catch them following, they peeked into the next corridor only to find it empty. Worse yet, there was no longer any sound coming from the woman's shoes.

"Where did she go?" asked Apple-Blossom her face showing how perplexed she now felt. She wasn't expecting an answer, but she got one.

Rex might have taken a moment to show off if such a concept ever occurred to a dog. Since it didn't, he simply employed his nose and walked to the door through which the woman had clearly gone.

"She went in there?" Apple-Blossom sought to confirm, placing her right ear against the door to hear the voices beyond.

Hearing multiple voices on the other side, all of them female, Apple-Blossom strained her hearing.

How Certain can you be?

"Oh, my, God! Those are her shoes!" squealed Selina. A detective chief inspector by rank and profession, she was not given to outbursts of panic. But her youngest – the unplanned surprise in her mid-forties – was missing, and inside her head, a voice was seeking permission to freak out.

Her daughter's shoes were lying abandoned in a narrow back hallway far from the reception on the other side of the palace. Worse yet, it looked as though they had been used to put out a fire.

Gary kept hold of his sister's hand for the support it might give.

Quizzing the soldiers who found them, two young men who were part of the palace ceremonial guard and deployed to scour the grounds the moment the little girl was reported missing, he asked, "There was no sign of the girl? This is exactly as you found them?"

The senior of the two soldiers, a lance corporal, if Gary was able to judge the rank correctly, nodded his head.

"We haven't touched them, sir."

"Spotted 'em when we turned into the hallway, we did," added his partner.

Gary and Selina were accompanied by two uniformed officers, additional security laid on by the Metropolitan Police for the day. They had expected a boring shift involving nothing but standing around. Now they had a potential child kidnapping on their hands and were being studious to suppress their glee.

"Why would she set a fire?" asked Constable Rivers.

Selina didn't like the question and rounded on the man who spoke.

"That was assumption, Rivers. Do you have any aspiration of making it into CID? Of being a detective? Huh? Because you'll fail instantly leaping to broad conclusions like that."

Gary tried to add some calm.

"He was just thinking out loud, Selina."

Backing away from the deranged mum who was also multiple ranks higher than he ever expected to get, Constable Rivers said, "Yeah, what he said."

Too worked up to calm down, Selina pointed out, "To me it looks as though she was putting a fire out."

Lance Corporal Shepherd, unconcerned about the police chain of command since it had no impact on him, stared at the charred remains.

"If she didn't start it, who did?"

Across the other side of the palace, Albert was with DI Munroe. They had more police officers with them as well as a team of palace staff. Those staff not directly involved in the reception were swiftly enlisted to help look for the little girl. Sent off in pairs with a photograph of Apple-Blossom Albert took from his phone, they were spreading out to cover as much ground as possible.

Albert and DI Munroe were more actively engaged in trying to confirm whether he had, in fact, seen Cody Williams. It was a disturbing, if unlikely, possibility DI Munroe hoped to clear up soon.

The soon came sooner than she expected when the old man by her side thrust out his right arm like an arrow.

"There! That's him over there!"

They were inside the palace still but moving along a corridor that looked out over a portion of the palace grounds.

What DI Munroe could see outside was the side entrance to the palace where the guests visiting for the day had been arriving less than an hour ago. The gate was quiet now, the barrier closed, but the pedestrian gate was still in use to allow egress and ingress for persons working within the palace, of which there were many.

Heading toward it was a man in palace uniform – one of the servers. He had a thin coat on over the top of his tunic and his head down, fast steps carrying him toward freedom.

On the radio in a flash, DI Munroe barked for the gates to be shut, employing a codeword that jolted the armed officers at the gate into action.

Unfortunately, they did that just after the man went through and came out the other side. He twisted his head to see what the commotion was and when one of the sentries shouted something at him, he took off running.

DI Munroe was also running, the officers in her company racing ahead, their longer legs carrying them more swiftly. Albert was left to bring up the rear, his days of sprinting long forgotten even though he considered himself to be capable and sprightly still.

By the time he got outside, Cody Williams was lying flat

on the pavement just outside the palace with two armed guards standing over him and a third about to haul him back onto his feet.

DI Munroe was halfway to the gate and waiting for Albert, her feet impatient.

"You're sure this is the man you saw earlier?" she quizzed.

A little out of breath and not entirely certain because, just like earlier, he only caught a fleeting glimpse, he nevertheless said, "Yes," in a confident tone.

In the street, cars were passing, the faces inside gawping and going slow to see the action unfolding outside the palace. DI Munroe saw multiple mobile phones in the hands of drivers and passengers alike. Whatever the outcome, she was going to have to explain today's events to her superiors and wondered if she would catch the blame if the palace had managed to hire a wanted murderer.

The pedestrian gate reopened before she got to it, Cody Williams pushed ahead of the armed police officers when they all came back inside the grounds.

"You're certain," DI Munroe pressed Albert again as they closed the final few yards.

Criminals

"Rex, they are talking about holding someone prisoner," hissed Apple-Blossom.

Rex heard the same thing, but wasn't sure what any of it meant. With his nose to the small gap at the base of the door, he could smell three women inside the room. Picking out their individual scents was easy for him. He knew they were of mating age though only one was currently in season. One wore a perfume he recognised and two used the same deodorant.

The one in season had eaten too much garlic the previous day and had a piece of rotting meat stuck in her teeth somewhere; Rex could smell her breath even from outside the room.

"What do you think we should do?" asked Apple-Blossom. There was something going on, that much she was certain of. It had to be something criminal too, but she couldn't hear enough to know what they were doing.

One of the women had talked about 'Rita' and 'Kimberly' two women who were somewhere else keeping hold of someone called 'Lionel' until after the job was done. It sounded like he wasn't going to be released until they had what they wanted, but then another of the women said something that confused Apple-Blossom.

"They really think they are going to be set free afterwards, don't they?" she sniggered.

Apple-Blossom could almost hear the shrug when the first woman replied.

"People cling to life. We gave them no choice. Cynthia either plays along or Rita and Kimberly cut her husband into pieces. Cynthia will do precisely as we demand so long as she thinks there is a chance she and her husband will make it through this alive."

"I know I've said it before, Kate …"

Apple-Blossom made a mental note of the name.

"… but this is a genius plan. We stand literally no chance of being caught. How did you come up with it?"

Apple-Blossom's chance to hear more was interrupted by the sound of approaching footsteps coming from inside the room. Someone was coming towards the door!

Grabbing Rex by his collar, she yanked and ran.

"Quick, Rex! Hide!"

Apple-Blossom's search for a hiding place quickly revealed a problem specific to corridors: there was nowhere to hide.

Holding Rex close by her side, Apple-Blossom would have been caught when the door opened if the same woman in the green dress thought once to look to her right.

The little girl hugged a door ten yards down the hallway, Rex tucked in tight by her legs. The doorframe provided a small alcove, which covered enough of their bodies that they went unnoticed. Just to be sure, Apple-Blossom kept hold of Rex's tail so he wouldn't wag it and give their position away.

The woman in the green dress was followed by another, and then another, three women all roughly the same size exiting the room one after the other. The last one made sure the door was shut before all three hurried away.

They spoke quietly, yet loud enough in the silent palace that their words reached Apple-Blossom's ears.

"Why haven't the fire alarms gone off, Shelley?" asked the one in the red dress. "You said you watched it ignite." Her tone was accusatory.

Shelley turned, giving Apple-Blossom a good look at the side of her face when she spat, "It was burning, all right, Leanne? Someone must have put it out."

"Oh, yeah?" argued Leanne. "If someone put it out before it set a chunk of the palace alight, how come this place isn't crawling with cops and stuff? Your job was to create the distraction. The fire would cause an evacuation and that was our way out."

The third woman, Apple-Blossom figured it must be 'Kate' had blonde hair and a blue dress and jacket, spoke over the top of the other two before they could really get into it.

"Ladies, that is enough. We should be thankful the plan has gone as well as it has so far. The fire and subsequent evacuation would have helped, but all is far from lost. We can set another, but for now I believe we need to return before we are missed. Cynthia will shortly be called forward to meet the king. Once that is over, there will be time to arrange our safe departure. Besides," she smiled at her accomplices just as they all turned the corner and were lost from sight, "no one will notice what we have done for days or even weeks. We can stroll out through the front gate and the police will wave us goodbye. I'm rather glad the fire didn't take."

The last words Apple-Blossom heard as their voices faded away was Shelley once again arguing that she set the fire. Her little heart beat hard inside her chest. She'd been scared before but never like this. It gave her new respect for her mummy and uncles who she knew to tackle criminals on a daily basis.

Rex gave the girl a nudge, leaving a wet dog nose mark on her right hand.

Apple-Blossom said, "Ewww, Rex," and wiped it on her dress.

The door to the room the women were in was now locked, barring their inspection so they could not know what might have been going on inside. That no longer mattered though. Apple-Blossom knew enough to report the crime and identify the three women. There were two more with Cynthia's husband, Lionel, and he was being held against his will until they completed whatever they were doing. Then they planned to kill both Cynthia and Lionel to cover their tracks – she had overheard it all.

Running back through the palace to find her mum and tell her everything, Apple-Blossom forgot one rather important detail: Her mum was frantic with worry and when reunited that emotion would dissolve to leave her hopping mad.

"Apple-Blossom!" Selina screeched, her consciousness spinning for a second such was her relief at seeing her little girl again.

"Mum!" Apple-Blossom cried out, thankful to have found her. She'd been so hopelessly lost, but Rex led her back to the people almost as if he knew the way.

Rex, of course, had simply followed his own scent back

the way they had come. They were almost back where they left Apple-Blossom's shoes when they ran into his human's pups. All three of them were together and very pleased to see him and the little girl.

Predictably, Selina hugged her daughter, squishing Apple-Blossom against her chest in a show of relief that drained the emotion from her. It didn't leave a void for long.

"What were you thinking!" she snapped, grabbing Apple-Blossom by both shoulders and pushing her back to arm's length so she could see her face.

"We found a crime happening, mummy," Apple-Blossom tried to explain.

Rex tugged at his lead – Randall had been quick to secure the dog and still couldn't work out how he had gotten free in the first place.

"It's this way," Rex barked. "You'll want to find someone with keys unless you feel like breaking down a door. I'm fairly sure it's locked."

"Whoa, boy." Randall reeled Rex back in. "You're not going anywhere. I'm not letting you out of my sight again."

"But the criminals were up to something down here," Rex barked again. "Where is my human? He will understand."

Apple-Blossom, able to speak in a language the adults could comprehend, was having no more luck than the dog.

"But, mummy …"

"No. I don't want to hear another word, young lady. You are in a lot of trouble. Wandering off at the palace …" Selina used an arm to indicate all the people around her. "Look at all the trouble you've caused. There are people all over the palace looking for you and your grandfather is supposed to be getting knighted by the king!"

"But, mummy, there really are criminals here. I heard

them talking about killing someone." Apple-Blossom was fighting hard not to cry. No one believed her and that stung. She could deal with being told off – that happened a lot anyway – but she needed them to listen, and they were refusing to do so.

At the palace's side gate the message that the little girl had been found reached the radio of DI Munroe just as she waited for Albert to confirm who they were looking at.

A Moment for Rex

"Ma'am, his identification and palace pass give his name as Gershwin George." The police officer who frisked and removed the man's wallet handed it over to DI Munroe.

She looked at it for a two-count, slowly lifting her head to compare the photograph to the man in custody and then around to look at Albert.

Gritting his teeth, Albert conceded, "It's not him."

"I'm not who?" Gershwin wanted to know.

Pressing Albert for more detail so she could clear this matter up and put it to bed, she asked, "Is this the man you saw earlier?"

Truthfully, Albert didn't know. Gershwin's features and hair, plus his body size, height, and shape were all very similar to Cody Williams. The differences were subtle, but now that he was scrutinising the man's face, they were also undeniable. Was it Gershwin he saw earlier? He could never know for sure, but the presence of such a close match standing four feet away made it hard to argue.

Reluctantly, Albert nodded his head. "Yes, probably."

"I need you to do better than that, Mr Smith. Is it still possible that Cody Williams was in the palace this morning?"

Looking confused Gershwin asked, "Who's Cody Williams?"

Albert wasn't happy about it. Wasn't happy at all. DI Munroe wanted a definitive answer, and he couldn't give one. Not in good conscience.

When he failed to answer, DI Munroe lifted her left arm and indicated with her head that the two of them needed to step away – she wanted a side bar.

"Look, Albert," DI Munroe chose to speak plainly. "I get it. You think you saw someone, but now we've found a person who looks just like the man you thought you saw. From what I understand reading the articles in the paper, you had a heck of a time out there trying to track down Earl Bacon. Cody Williams is one of those guys who managed to get away and that must be hard for you. To know he's still out there."

Albert listened, uncertain where she was going with her line of reasoning.

"I need to close this or we need to keep scouring the palace until we can be utterly certain Cody Williams was never here. You came here to be knighted by the king and the process of presenting people to his royal highness is already in motion. If I don't get you back inside and reunite you with your family soon, you might miss out on your big day. This is not the sort of thing a person wants to receive through the post a month after the event. Now, can we agree that you saw Gershwin George and leave it at that?"

Albert drew in a deep breath and huffed it out slowly. She was being kind, but at the same time talking to him like he was getting old and less in control of his mental faculties than he might believe. It happened a lot at his age and the biggest problem it generated was self-doubt. Was his brain getting a little spotty? Were his eyes playing tricks on him?

Starting to feel like he wanted to get back to his children and beginning to feel thoroughly embarrassed, Albert made sure his voice came out strong and sure when he apologised for wasting DI Munroe's time and thanked her for giving credence to his concerns.

It was the right stance to take; his decades of experience dictating that he knew what to say in such circumstances though it was the first time he wasn't the one filling DI Munroe's shoes.

Gershwin was released and sent on his way with a few words of encouragement from the officers who tackled him to the ground.

Excitement over, DI Munroe led Albert back through the palace, arriving in the reception room to find he'd missed his slot to be presented to the king. The organisers merely skipped over him, the monarch none the wiser, yet Albert's reappearance meant they were able to slot him back into the line up of individuals waiting to approach the throne.

"Here, Dad," Randall passed Rex's lead to his father. "You'll want this."

Albert noted Apple-Blossom's face.

"Is she all right?" he asked Selina.

Still angry and riding the wave of mixed emotions losing and finding a child will always muster, Selina sighed heavily.

"She's fine, Dad. Just upset about being told off."

"No, I'm not!" snapped Apple-Blossom tearfully, almost stamping her foot in the process. "I'm upset because you won't listen to me."

A man in a suit stepped up next to Albert, an electronic tablet in his hand and earpiece on a wire in his right ear.

"Mr Smith," he beamed, checking his list. "And Rex Harrison, no less. I believe this is the first dog ever on the monarch's birthday honours list."

"Well, dogs have received medals for gallantry before," supplied Randall. "Quite a few of them, in fact, during the first and second world wars."

"Is that so?" beamed the man with the tablet. "Well, you are up next, Mr Smith, soon to be Sir Albert."

Albert mumbled, "Good Lord," and rolled his eyes.

Rex nudged his leg, and when he looked down he saw his dog staring back at him.

"Listen to the little girl," Rex advised, his little chuffing noises something Albert had come to recognise even if he could not understand them.

Selina was trying to shush her child who continued to complain about something to do with 'criminals and someone being held hostage'.

Directly in front of Albert, a man he recognised from the television was about to be called forward. He could see over his head to the king at the end of a plush red carpet. He looked thoroughly regal, waiting with his sword to bestow verbally the honours each individual was considered worthy to merit.

The person currently kneeling before the king was the gymnast Randall was chatting up from the moment they first arrived. Albert wanted to ask his youngest if he'd gotten her number; just to distract himself from the fluttering of nerves he felt, but there was something about the intensity of Rex's stare and the things Apple-Blossom was saying.

The man with the tablet sent the TV personality down

to meet the king just as the gymnast exited to the right, then called Albert forward — he was next.

Rex nudged him again.

Albert met his dog's gaze once more. He might not have been certain he'd really seen Cody Williams, but there was one thing he knew for sure: his dog was something special. Rex was trying to tell him something and over the months they were on the road together, Albert learned to listen.

Coming down into a crouch — far less easy a manoeuvre than it used to be — Albert ruffled the fur around Rex's neck.

"Did Apple-Blossom see something?" he asked.

Rex bounced from his sitting position onto his feet and licked Albert's chin.

Thinking fast, Albert asked, "Are there criminals here? Is someone in trouble?"

"Did Timmy fall down the well?" asked Gary, his tone mocking. "What are you doing, Dad? This is your moment."

"Is it?" Albert asked, his eyes never leaving Rex's. Reaching up to unclip his dog's lead, he said, "I think perhaps it's about to be Rex's."

Free of his tether, Rex backed up half a yard, uncertain what he was expected to do next.

"Sixty seconds," said the man with the tablet. Ahead of them, the TV personality was rising and about to leave.

Taking a single calming breath, Albert said, "Show me, Rex."

Dementia or Attention?

Rex barked once, the sound echoing through the grand hall they were standing just inside. The sound brought the king's head up to see what was happening just as Rex turned and ran.

Gary uttered an audible expletive, his cheeks colouring when he realised how loud the word came out.

Albert ran after Rex, stopping only to grab Apple-Blossom's hand.

"Come on, granddaughter! Show me what you found."

Behind them, as Albert ran down the side of the great hall to exit ahead of the bewildered looking TV presenter, astonished cries erupted. The man with the tablet tried to queue up the next person as fast as he could and Albert's three children, momentarily left behind when their father took off, had to run to catch up.

Feeling the monarch's eyes tracking his movement, Randall blurted, "Terribly sorry, your royalness," and raced from the room.

Outside, they spotted their father. Albert had already grabbed a cop and was yelling for him to contact DI Munroe.

Running behind his dog, who kept stopping to make sure the humans were following, Albert raced away.

"Sir!" the cop yelled. "Sir, that's a restricted area. You can't go down there!"

Unperturbed, Albert called over his shoulder, "That's why I need you! Keep up, young man."

Unsure what to do, but knowing the dog had gone under the 'restricted area' sign and was gone before he could do anything about it, Constable Copley also gave chase. Using his radio to do as Albert asked, he raised DI Munroe.

"Again?" she replied, struggling to believe the old man was up to no good for a second time so soon after she returned him to his family. Was he suffering from dementia or was this all a play to get more attention?

"He said something about criminals and murder, Ma'am. What should I do?" Copley asked a little breathlessly as he jogged to keep up.

Frustrated, and wanting to be left alone for five minutes to enjoy her cup of tea and two digestive biscuits – her ration of sweet stuff for the day – Munroe huffed that he should follow the old man, prove he was chasing ghosts and bring him back to the reception room. DI Munroe was going to make sure the old man got knighted and gleefully kick him out of the palace. There was a second champagne reception, with the king this time, held in the gardens behind the palace when all the knighthoods had been handed out.

Well, Albert Smith had just forfeited his right to attend it.

She changed her tune fifteen minutes later when she heard what Constable Copley had found.

Debt of Gratitude

"Dozens of them," Copley reported, meeting DI Munroe outside in the hallway when he heard her coming.

Apple-Blossom bore a smug look, but was keeping quiet about being right. Albert had taken her to one side when Copley had someone bring keys to open the door Rex kept nudging with his head. His advice to loftily assume the higher position of the person in the right would force her mother to apologise for not believing her claims. Apple-Blossom wanted to point out how she 'Told you so', but her grandfather's words rang in her ears while the cops examined the empty frames.

The room was an art store. Filled with oil paintings – Albert guessed they were old and valuable – the canvasses were missing in every direction one cared to look.

"This is unbelievable," DI Munroe murmured. Spinning to face Albert, she demanded, "You saw guests at the reception coming in here today?"

"Not me," Albert shook his head. "Rex and Apple-Blossom must be credited with solving this crime."

DI Munroe jinked an eyebrow. "The dog? And the little girl?"

"I'm not *that* little," argued Apple-Blossom, a deep frown creasing her forehead. "I'm third tallest in my class, thank you very much." She wanted to point out that DI Munroe was the shortest adult in the room by a fair margin, but chose to get to the point instead. "I can show you who I saw, if you like. There were three of them, but they have two more accomplices at another location and I'm just guessing this part, but I think they probably have a fourth person here."

DI Munroe choked on a laugh. This was a better report than she got from half of her subordinates.

"I suppose you know their names too," she joked.

"Only their first names. They never said their last names." Apple-Blossom reeled off what she knew, shocking her mother with the detail amassed, and making sure to credit Rex for all his help.

Rex wagged his tail each time he was mentioned.

It took less than a minute to confirm the 'Cynthia' Apple-Blossom heard referenced was none other than Cynthia Yang, a famous thriller writer and the previous year's Booker Prize recipient. She was the only Cynthia at the event and a quick internet search confirmed her husband's name to be Lionel.

Whoever DI Munroe was talking to via her radio, the message came back that Mrs Yang was about to be presented to the king. The alphabetical list of persons being honoured was almost at an end.

Coordinating things as they walked back through the palace, walked not ran because DI Munroe determined there was no need to rush now. There were officers on their way to Cynthia Yang's house where they would innocently knock on the door, yank the person who answered from it, and storm the premises.

The three women Apple-Blossom described were confirmed to be waiting with the writer, one away from being next to meet the king.

They left a man called Sir Cuthbert to review the missing artwork. He was horrified upon seeing the state of the room, and had assistants on their way to help him catalogue what had been taken.

It was for the sake of the artwork that the ladies with Cynthia Yang were not tackled to the floor. DI Munroe wanted to take them cleanly and in one swift swoop which dictated the best chance to do so was when Cynthia walked alone through the hall to be presented to the king.

They waited for that to happen, Albert, Rex, Apple-Blossom, and Albert's three children all watching from the wings when armed officers moved in ahead of DI Munroe to surround the three rather rotund ladies.

The truth behind their size came to light just a few moments later when a light frisk revealed the missing oil paintings secured in tubes beneath their bulbous dresses. The three ladies had what are rather indelicately known as 'fat suits' on their top halves. Covered by their jackets and hair, there wasn't that much of the fake flesh on display. With a little makeup and high-necked dresses, it was easy to see why no one noticed they didn't look quite right.

From the waist down the women all had supporting frames to fill the dresses and it was inside there that they each had more than a dozen priceless oil paintings rolled and stashed.

The fourth member of their team had been left to stick with Cynthia while the other three perpetrated their crime.

The fire was supposed to send the palace security scurrying and cause an evacuation that would help to cover their escape.

Unaware that she was being rescued until after the king granted her knighthood, Mrs Yang was overcome with concern for her husband. When the call came to confirm he was with the police and unharmed, she almost collapsed.

The all-female gang invaded the Yang house the previous evening, forcing Cynthia to make last minute changes to her four permitted guests. She'd only been taking her husband – they were a childless couple – and she had no idea what they wanted, only that they threatened to skewer Lionel if she didn't do exactly as they said.

It was just when the quad of women were being led away in cuffs that a familiar clearing of a throat made everyone spin about to see who was behind them.

"I believe one had missed out on something interesting today," said King Charles.

A swift round of bowing and curtseying took place.

Rex watched the humans with confusion.

"What are you all doing?" he asked, wagging his tail in case this was the start of a game they were all going to play.

Albert lifted his head to find the king's hand was held out for him to shake.

"One believes a debt of gratitude is owed."

"Not to me, Your Majesty," Albert repeated an earlier claim. "This was the work of my granddaughter, Apple-Blossom, and Rex who has an uncanny knack for finding people doing things they ought not to be doing."

The king made a show of thanking Apple-Blossom, posing so an official photographer could take a picture.

"Now then," King Charles came out of the kneeling

crouch he'd assumed to be snapped with the little girl, "One believes there is a final matter of business to which one must attend before I can get out of this wretchedly heavy cloak."

The man with the tablet reappeared, snapping his fingers at people so they could take their places. Once the monarch was ready, Albert led Rex down the red carpet where they were both granted honours. Albert knew he was being bestowed with Knight Commander of the British Empire, but was surprised when the king unexpectedly chose to bestow the same honour upon Rex.

"One feels today's actions warrant it," said the king by way of explanation.

Feeling like he was walking on air, despite previously and continuously stating that he possessed no interest in the honour, Albert strolled out into the palace gardens with the king chatting amiably at his side.

"Do you have a plus one to bring to the wedding, Sir Albert?" King Charles asked.

Sir Albert? That was going to take some getting used to.

Blinking, he realised what the king had just said.

"The wedding, Your Highness?"

"Yes, Sir Albert. I rather think you should come along. My youngest son, Marcus, has orchestrated a less lavish affair than either of his brothers, but I believe it will be an enjoyable event. Will you be able to attend?"

The king gave Albert the date, oblivious to the elbow nudging going on behind them where Albert's children were reeling from the conversation they could not help but overhear.

One thing Albert knew for sure was that he would be free to attend. Weddings were not his thing, but when the King of England invites you …

They descended some stone steps to the garden where

palace staff were once again passing among the throng of guests with food and drinks.

High above them in a window overlooking the gardens from the north wing of the palace, Cody Williams stared through a set of binoculars to the people below.

Albert Smith? How on earth was Albert Smith here?

Police Dog

DAY ONE

Rubber Stamp

Sergeant Gruber scratched his head. What was he supposed to do in this situation?

"You can't pass him," insisted Mike. "Dave is still off work because of him."

Jason agreed, "Mike's right. You can't pass him."

This was the crux of the problem facing Sergeant Gruber – he knew that he really shouldn't pass Rex Harrison. The oversized German Shepherd dog was a menace. Dave was off work because Rex insisted on avoiding the pads when he went after his handlers in the drills.

It was as if the dog saw them as a sort of soft or easy target and thus beneath him. Getting bitten wasn't a new thing, of course, the guys accepted it was just part of the job. Sooner or later, a dog was going to miss the padding you were gamely offering for them to bite. Rex though, Rex chose to ignore the pads.

He'd bitten twelve instructors. Twelve. It was twelve times as many as any other dog in the history of the academy. Dave had got the worst of it. Not content to go for an ankle when a padded arm was offered, Rex chose to bite Dave's trousers.

Not the back of Dave's trousers, let's be clear about that. No, that might have been forgivable. Dave's colleagues were still up in arms about it. Clearly.

Sergeant Gruber last spoke to Dave yesterday. He was recovering … mostly. The bigger issue, so far as Dave saw it, was that his wife didn't know what he was making all the fuss about and even made a joke that the dog must have a jolly good aim.

Dave's concerns aside, what Dave believed to be the bigger issue wasn't the bigger issue at all. The bigger issue was that Sergeant Gruber was under pressure to deliver trained police dogs and no matter how many he produced, it was never enough.

"You've had two hundred recruits this year!" Sergeant Gruber recalled his most recent unpleasant conversation. "How is that you have such a high fail rate?" his boss had demanded to know.

Charlie Gruber would happily explain to anyone the complexities of training a dog … any dog, to do all the things that was required of a modern police canine, but the problem was that the people he needed to explain it to just didn't want to listen.

The Metropolitan Police wanted police dogs. They wanted them now, and he sometimes wondered how long it would take them to notice if he sent them a poorly trained goat in a disguise.

Ultimately, he knew that if he failed Rex Harrison as his instructors expected, his boss would scrutinise the results and question his judgement. It really was a career decision he was being forced to make.

Rex Harrison hadn't just passed every test, he'd aced

them. The dog had an air of superiority that made it seem as though he was looking down on his human handlers. If you watched him, which Sergeant Gruber had on many occasions, you found yourself questioning whether the dog was watching the humans around him with disappointment.

"You're going to, aren't you," accused Mike. "You weak sell out."

"Hey!" Charlie Gruber had known Mike for years, and they had never fallen out. Heck, Mike came to Charlie's daughter's wedding. Mike was toeing the line right now though.

Scowling a warning at every face in the room, Sergeant Gruber picked up his stamp, rubbed it in the ink pad, and slammed it down on Rex Harrison's paperwork.

He was a pass whether the instructors liked it or not.

Day One

"This is day one on the job, Rex," remarked Constable Ruari McGee, the human holding his harness. "I have to get used to you just as much as you need to get used to me. You've had all the training and today we get to find out if you can cut it in the real world."

Rex Harrison looked up at the human holding his harness. The man was chattering away, his words coming too fast for Rex to capture them all. However, none of his key command words were being said, so Rex wasn't paying him much attention. Instead, Rex was sifting the air.

"Obey my commands, come to heel when I call, and above all don't embarrass me. If you can do that, we'll get along just fine," the man continued to talk, the words going over Rex's head. "We're just going on a routine patrol today; nothing exciting. This will be all we do for the next few weeks. When I'm confident you are ready for something more, you will get the chance to prove yourself. Until then, the older, more experienced dogs will take the lead."

Rex frowned a little, questioning why he needed to defer to the older dogs, but held back the comment in his head.

They set off, Constable McGee leading Rex away from the van they travelled in. Rex wasn't a fan of the cage he was expected to clamber into each time – it was too restricting on his bulky frame, but the human had made it as comfortable as he could by adding a padded blanket to the base.

Nevertheless pleased to be out of it and moving, Rex continued to sample the air around him. London's streets were awash with scents that fought for superiority. There were three ... no four rats in the alleyway he'd just passed. Rex could smell their individual odours as surely as reading a book. They were feasting upon an abandoned slice of pepperoni pizza and were being stalked by a pair of alley cats they were yet to detect.

Ahead of him was a laundromat place next to a drycleaner's and beyond them was a public house. The public house was closed, it being not long after breakfast time, but Rex could smell where beer and other alcoholic liquids had soaked into the wooden floorboards over the decades.

They were close to Tower Hamlets, a dingy suburb of London, patrolling the streets with no great purpose other than to maintain a police presence. The Commissioner of the Metropolitan Police believed community policing was at the heart of reducing crime. People should know there were officers nearby for the assurance and sense of security it gave them. The unspoken subtext was that it made those considering a crime have seconds thoughts. Arguably that was even more helpful to the community.

They walked a rectangular route, Constable McGee stopping to chat with three different pairs of old ladies who wanted to meet 'his handsome dog' and some kids who were skateboarding where they ought not to during school hours when they should be in class. They also stopped when they came across a drunk/drugged person who was walking the streets in socks and a shirt, but no trousers.

Dealing with the disorientated and confused man in his late thirties took up half an hour, an ambulance coming to take him once McGee was content the man posed no threat.

They were almost back at the van when the call came over his radio.

Rex's ears pricked up – they had a crook to catch!

Griping because he didn't want to go back into the cage, Rex complained, "*We can go faster on foot at this time of day. It's only down the road in Limehouse. You'll get stuck at the junction. Did you not see the traffic there earlier?*"

Constable McGee had no idea what the dog's noises were all about, and gave Rex's skull a shove so he could close the cage door.

"This will be interesting for you, Rex," McGee said as he lowed the van's rear door. "We'll just go there and observe."

"*Observe?*" Rex couldn't see why he wasn't expected to add value and continued to mutter all the way there. Mostly he complained about the time it was taking because they were stuck in traffic at the junction just as he predicted.

Finally out of the van and able to join the other dogs at the scene, Rex stopped to look at a footprint at the edge of a puddle. He gave it a sniff, leaning his weight away from his handler until he could get a good sample.

Forced to move on, he looked around. They were approaching a small, independent hardware shop. Rex's nose detected the preservative oil used to coat the machines and tool inside, plus the heavy, base smell he always got from new steel. He picked up hundreds of other smells and strained to get inside where he knew the other dogs with their humans had congregated.

Dragging Constable McGee through the door, his nose picked up a scent that didn't belong.

"*Oh, look, it's the new kid,*" huffed Nelson, a four-year-old veteran German Shepherd. Rex had met him and most of the other service dogs a few days ago when he left the academy. Too enthusiastic and exuberant, Rex had instantly been given the cold shoulder by almost every dog on the team. Rex wanted to get out and catch bad guys, believing he had the skills and the smarts to be successful on the capital's streets.

His contemporaries thought otherwise. They'd seen it and heard it all before. Most new dogs were just like him. Pumped full of daft ideas from their time at the academy, they had no idea how things worked in the real world.

Standing next to Nelson was another German Shepherd, this one a three-year-old called Roy Orbison. Though it was completely lost on the dogs, the instructors at the academy got to name the batches of puppies and had long ago elected to theme the intakes. Roy Orbison was in a tranche of dogs all named after American pop stars of the sixties.

Roy sniggered at Nelson's comment. "*We can probably relax then. Give Rex five minutes and he'll have solved the whole thing.*"

Rex chose to ignore them, sitting obediently at Constable McGee's feet. While his human talked to his colleagues, Rex closed his eyes and sifted his way through the scents carried on the air. Above his head one of the officers was talking to the owner of the hardware place.

"So you didn't get a good look at his face?" asked Constable Kate Spalding.

The store manager had been robbed, the thief getting away with a van load of new tools and equipment, plus the contents of the till.

"Sorry, no. I was in the storeroom at the back and whoever it was that robbed the place locked me in."

Kate asked, "You said there was over a thousand pounds in the till, what were you doing with that kind of money at this time of the day? Aren't most of your transactions by card these days?"

"Well, yes," the man replied, sounding apologetic. "I guess I've always carried a big float. It makes it easy if people do want to pay with cash."

Another of the officers, Constable Harry Kemp sought to confirm, "You're the manager, not the owner, correct?"

Again the man sounded apologetic when he said, "That's right. I'll have to call the boss and let him know. He'll not be pleased. This isn't the first time we've been hit like this."

"No," remarked Kate. "It's the third time in six months, the method and nature of the robbery the same each time. Each time it occurs when it is only you at the store and you always get locked in the storeroom."

"That's not true," protested the store manager. "Last time I was locked in the toilet."

Kate pressed on, "How come the owner hasn't paid to fit a camera system so we might stand a chance of catching the thief behind it?"

"Oh, there are cameras," explained the store manager. "Buuut, I sometimes forget to turn them on."

Nelson, looking to have a little fun at Rex's expense, asked, "*Solved it yet?*"

Rex opened his eyes and stood up. "*Solved it? No, not yet. However, the man we are looking for has been near fish today, but he doesn't work on a boat because the scent of the river we can all detect is coming from it, not from inside this room. I figure that means the fish market. The nearest one to here is Billingsgate just a mile or so from where we are standing.*"

Nelson and Roy Orbison looked at each other. They had smelled all the things Rex was smelling, but hadn't even attempted to add the clues together.

Rex continued, "*Also, he is single because there is no trace of a female human's smell mingled in with his and he's badly overweight.*"

"*Overweight?*" questioned Nelson. "*How on earth can you tell that from his smell?*"

"*Yeah,*" agreed Roy, challenging Rex to have an answer.

Rex would have given a sad shake of his head if such a gesture meant anything to a dog. Instead, he raised an eyebrow.

"*Did you not notice the footprint in the mud outside? It rained for the first time in days after closing time last night so the puddle and thus the footprint are fresh. The business only opened an hour ago and it doesn't look like this place does a lot of trade,*" he commented, looking about at the dated and drab interior. "*The shoe that left the print is a size thirteen extra wide. If you don't believe me, go check for yourself. The footprint also stinks of fish and ... something else. Something greasy. I'm having trouble pinpointing what it is, but I'm heading to Billingsgate Market to see if I can find it there. If the scents overlap, I'll have found where our perpetrator has been. Given the depth of scent, I think we can assume he is there regularly and will be back there soon enough.*"

Nelson and Roy Orbison were gawping now, their lower jaws hanging open in shock. Gathering himself, and remembering that he was one of the more experienced dogs and thus expected to train and guide Rex in 'the way things work around here', Nelson chose to scoff.

"*You're going to Billingsgate Market, are you? What if your human has other plans?*"

Rex tilted his head to one side, thinking the question was a strange one to pose.

"*Then I'll go without him.*"

Nelson and Roy fell into a fit of laughter.

Kate, Harry, and Ruari looked down at their dogs.

"What got into them?" asked Harry, tugging on Roy's lead to make him stop the odd chuffing noise.

Kate had taken a statement from the store manager, Anthony Stone, and would file a report. There were no witnesses to the robbery and therefore nothing much the police could do. The report would be followed up to see if it could be linked to any other crimes in the area, but that would be handled by the detectives, not by the dog handlers who only got to respond this time because they were the closest units in the area.

Rex felt a tug on his lead.

Constable McGee said, "Come along, Rex. Let's get back in the van. I think we'll head back to the station and see what is going on there."

"*The station?*" Rex questioned. "*But didn't you smell the fish? I know human's have a terrible sense of smell, but come on. It was obvious!*"

Nelson and Roy called after him as they were led to their vans. "*Good luck catching the bad guy,*" they laughed.

Disappointed with his human's lack of interest, confused about what they were doing if they weren't going to follow the trail of clues the criminal left behind, and pushed to act irrationally by Nelson and Roy's goading, Rex decided to do what he knew was right.

Doing What is Right

Ruari opened the van and slipped off Rex's harness.

"In you get, boy," he clicked his fingers and pointed into the cage.

Rex took one look at it, turned his head to catch Nelson's eye, winked, and was gone.

The shout of outrage came as no surprise, but Constable McGee's flailing arms never even got close to stopping Rex as he neatly sidestepped his human's legs and started running. Able to go from stationary to full speed in just a few bounds, Rex shot past the hardware store, rounded the corner, and tore down Ming Street.

All three police dog vans were chasing him before he got to the Limehouse Link Road, however keeping him in sight and catching him were two very different things.

Rex knew they were back there and acknowledged that it was a good thing. He could find where the criminal had been, but that wasn't the same as catching him. Furthermore, even if he did find the robber and took him down,

Rex couldn't perform an arrest – he needed a human for that.

In his van, Constable McGee had some choice words to share with the world. Dogs fresh from the academy were supposed to be super obedient. He was going to catch merry hell from his boss when Rex's escape became public knowledge. Which it would. Worse yet, having transferred to the Met only recently because his wife took a job in the city, he was still on a kind of virtual probation himself.

He hadn't wanted to move, but his wife made it clear she was going with or without him when she got the job offer. He'd supported her for years while she studied, and now she earned five times what he did and decided she could call the shots.

With Canary Wharf to his right, Rex ran at a steady pace. He got a few looks from pedestrians as he went by and scared a bunch of seagulls who were squabbling over a bacon roll someone had dropped. Rex snagged it without breaking stride and swallowed it whole as the seagulls swarmed overhead and swore revenge.

He ran on, the stench from the fish market becoming stronger with each passing yard. The traffic on Upper Bank Street was too heavy for him to cross but a pedestrian overpass provided the safe route he needed.

The police officers in their vans couldn't follow him and had been tracking his progress as best they could from the Limehouse Link. Seeing his dog finally slow as he reached the outer fringes of Billingsgate Market, Constable McGee messaged Kate and Harry – he was turning off to go on foot if he could.

Oblivious to what his handler was doing, Rex stopped running. At a slow trot, he made his way up to the entrance gate to the market grounds but there he stopped.

A human was looking at him.

Actually, the human, a security guard for the market called Arran Renfroe was looking at the jacket the dog wore. Along the German Shepherd's flanks it read 'Police' in big, shiny letters. Arran couldn't see a police officer anywhere, but if the dog was here then the handler couldn't be too far away.

Was it one of those sniffer dogs that could pick up the scent of drugs? Arran had a joint in his top pocket and the dog was staring right at it.

Rex could indeed smell the marijuana in the man's pocket but was paying it no attention. He had a one-track mind right now, and it was trying to figure out whether he needed to venture into the market or not. The scent of fish had brought him this far, but it was the other smell, the greasy smell that was proving hard to locate.

It wasn't a smell he associated with the fish market, but it had to be close by.

Hearing the squeal of tyres to his rear, Rex twitched his head around to look over his shoulder. His human counterpart was getting out of his van, and he looked annoyed.

In truth, Constable McGee looked apoplectic with rage, but Rex wasn't able to pick up the fine definitions between different human emotions. Either way, Rex hadn't found the source of the robber's scent yet, so no matter how loudly Constable McGee shouted, Rex wasn't coming back.

He picked up his pace, running past the entrance to the fish market which left Arran breathing a sigh of relief.

The front façade of the market stretched on for a hundred yards, but coming to the far corner, Rex caught the first trace of the greasy smell in his nostrils and doubled his pace.

He knew what it was now, and it was going to be so easy to find!

Human Weaknesses

Constable McGee had been out of his van and running to get the harness back on Rex when the dog took off again. Fruitlessly, he screamed the dog's name and chased after him. He got five yards before he hit the brakes and ran back to the van.

Kate and Harry were both staring at their new colleague through their windscreens, disbelief and amusement fighting to be the dominant emotion colouring their expressions. Ruari was the new guy and even though he was an experienced dog handler, he was yet to prove himself. The wider team were going to love being regaled with this story.

Stopping the video she was shooting on her phone, Kate put her van back in gear and followed when Harry pulled out behind Ruari again.

Following his nose, Rex changed direction only once before he found what he was looking for. A snack shack sitting at the edge of the wharf stank of grease and fish. It also held the unmistakable, undeniable odour of the same man Rex could smelled in the hardware store.

Though humans appear to be blithely unaware, they all smell completely different. Better than fingerprints, the unique combination of sweat, diet, individual choice of soap and products carrying a scent all join together to generate a signature any dog could follow.

Rex ran around the small wooden building looking for a way in.

"Rex!" bellowed Constable McGee, stomping toward his dog. He said some other things that are entirely unprintable.

"*Ah, jolly good*," barked Rex. "*I can't tell if he's in there right now, but this is his place and the goods he stole from the hardware place are definitely inside.*" Pointing at the door with his nose, Rex expected his human to open it and was greatly shocked when instead Constable McGee chose to snap his harness into place and begin dragging him away.

"I'm sending you back to the academy," Ruari threatened. "I've never had a dog ran away before. Never. What on earth was going through your mind?"

Rex dug his feet in. "*I was thinking it was a good idea to catch the criminal,*" he whined. He wanted to bark and snap at his dopey human, but knew that would be considered bad behaviour.

Harry and Kate were both out of their vans too, and taking their dogs out because both Nelson and Roy Orbison were going nuts.

The moment Nelson's harness was on, he had his nose to the ground and was pulling his human across the tarmac. When Roy did likewise, both Harry and Kate went with them.

"Hey, Ruari," Kate called out. The new guy was

fighting with his dog, trying to get him back to the van while the dog clearly wanted him to look at the snack shack.

By the time Ruari finally looked up, Harry was already at the shack and peering through the window.

"Well, I'll be," he choked out a surprised laugh.

Curious, Kate caught up to him and looked too. Her reaction was one of awe.

"Ruari, you have to come see this."

Nelson and Roy Orbison didn't know what to make of it. They could smell the same man who'd been in the hardware store, but neither of them had thought to pursue it themselves. They hadn't really given it any thought at all. Their humans hadn't asked them to do anything; the suspect was believed to have escaped in a motorised vehicle, so they were not going to be tasked with tracking his scent overland.

Truthfully, they felt a little embarrassed that the new dog, the young pup as they still thought of him, had found the missing property so easily.

With her radio, Kate advised dispatch that they were forcing entry to the snack shack and gave Harry the nod to break the glass in the door.

Constable McGee, bringing Rex with him despite wanting to lock him in the back of the van, couldn't believe his eyes. Gawping at his dog, he asked, "How did you know?"

Rex twitched one eyebrow and tilted his head.

"*I used my nose, dummy.*"

His comment brought a snigger from Nelson and Roy, but before either could comment, Rex was pulling on his human handler's arm again. Rex's nose was twitching. Now that the glass was broken and the air inside was drifting out, there was something ...

Kate was relaying what they had found to dispatch. Explaining that the snack shack's owner was nowhere in sight, she tasked the person she was talking to with finding out who owned the food outlet. When her own dog, Nelson tugged at her arm, she twisted her torso around to see what he was doing.

Nelson was trying to get a better sniff.

Rex was being held back by his handler and couldn't get close enough to properly sniff for himself. However, he'd caught a whiff on the breeze and already knew they weren't done yet. A nod from Nelson when he picked up the same scent was all the confirmation he needed.

"*So what do we do?*" asked Roy, snorting in a noseful of air from the shack to find the scent for himself. They never would have found it if Roy's handler hadn't broken in, but there was no denying the smell was there now.

It was strong too. Too strong to have come with the stolen gear and that meant it was fresh.

Nelson said, "*We wait for them to figure it out. They'll catch this guy, and they will figure the rest of it out from there. They always do. It's not our job to solve the crimes. We find things when we are asked to.*" Nelson felt like the ground was shifting under his feet and he wasn't sure he liked it. The new dog had done something no other dog had ever done – followed a bunch of random clues to solve a crime.

Rex sighed. "*Really? That's your plan. Hope the humans figure it out? Look at them. They're not even sniffing in the right place.*"

"*What else would you have us do?*" Roy demanded, not used to being talked down to by pups whose whiskers had barely finished growing.

Rex bunched his muscles. "*Well, I think we should help the humans. Isn't that our job? They have the things that they are good at doing,*" Rex conceded generously. "*I couldn't have broken that window to get inside. They also have their weaknesses,"* he pointed out.

Nelson couldn't argue with that. *"He's not wrong. It drives me scatty when my human won't use her nose to find things."*

"Exactly," said Rex, getting ready to do something he already knew would be unpopular. *"The only question is whether the two of you are with me?"* Rex watched Nelson and Roy look inward at each other. *"Or are you just a bit too old now?"*

Not waiting for a response to his taunt, Rex shot forward. Driving off with his back feet, he snapped his human's arm in a direction it didn't want to go and broke the tight grip Ruari was keeping on the harness.

Constable McGee was pulled off balance and fell. Landing with an undignified 'Oooofff' and kicking up a cloud of dust, he got to watch as Rex shot forward three yards and stop. There, the brand new police dog spun around to prance excitedly.

"Come on!" he barked at Roy and Nelson, and much to their own surprise, both dogs did exactly as Rex had. Breaking free of their handler's, they ran after Rex who was already pivoting back to face the way he wanted to go.

With curse words and ignored commands being hurled at their backs, all three police dogs rounded the corner of the fish market and vanished from sight. Ruari slapped Harry's hand away when it was offered to help him up. He was altogether too angry to see sense.

"That dog is a menace!" he growled. "I don't care what the boss says. I don't care what my wife says. I am not working with Rex Harrison for another minute. I'm going to catch that dog. I'll ... I'll run him over if I have to, but he's going back to the station, and I'm done with him."

The Dog Knew

Arran, his heartrate back to normal, had been replaced at the front gate and was sneaking across the road to get a coffee. There was a little place that backed onto the DLR rail line. Away from everyone, he could smoke his joint in peace. It would make the rest of the day a breeze.

Patting his uniform's top left pocket to reassure himself the rolled weed was still there, he froze when he heard the sound of claws on the pavement. They were coming his way and they were moving fast.

Twisting around to face the approaching danger, his breath caught when he saw it was not the one dog like before, but three! There were three police dogs streaking toward him like they were in a race to see who could bring him down first.

Panicked fingers ripped the joint from his pocket and he threw it at the street as he backed away.

"Here!" he yelled. "It's not mine anyway! I was just ... I was holding it for a friend. An acquaintance really. In fact, I don't even like the guy."

His back hit the security railings surrounding the fish market and he stopped, his eyes wide in horror as the three dogs bore down on him.

They raced by, never giving him a second glance and with a gasp of air, Arran breathed yet another sigh of relief.

They weren't after him at all.

The joint was still on the pavement, and now that his nerves were frayed, he felt he needed it more than ever. Just as he stooped to pick it up, three police dog handler vans power slid around the corner and began powering up the road toward him. All three hit their strobe lights and sirens to clear the road and that was the last straw for Arran.

Stomping on the marijuana to destroy the evidence, he hustled back inside the confines of the fish market.

Quarter of a mile away, Rex, Nelson, and Roy Orbison were panting hard but none of them were going to be the first to slow down. They had crooks to catch and though they wouldn't admit it openly, Roy and Nelson were feeling more invigorated than they had in years.

They were a little concerned about the repercussions of running off, but it was too late to return now. They needed to see it through.

Two minutes later, panting harder than ever, they arrived back at the hardware store.

"Now what?" gasped Roy, thankful he could slow down.

Rex slowed to a walk too. They were in the carpark outside the hardware store staring at the building. They could hear their handlers, the wailing sirens filling the air as they bore down on the dogs' position.

Getting enough oxygen in his lungs to speak, Rex said, "Now we have to find them."

In the vans, Kate was leading. She was talking to Ruari

and Harry, all three trying to guess where the dogs had gone since they weren't able to keep track of them the whole way.

"They must have gone back to where we started," she guessed.

Ruari didn't see why that would be true. "Why would that be more likely than anywhere else?" he questioned. He was all for just going back to the station without the dogs.

Kate frowned, her forehead forming deep creases. "Where else could they have gone? Your dog ran directly from the hardware store to where the stolen goods had been stashed. I know it sounds daft, but I think he knows something."

Ruari spat out a laugh. "The dog knows something? What? Like he's following the clues to catch the bad guy? Can I rename him Sherlock Bones?"

Kate chose not to reply, and Harry stayed silent. The new guy was not making any friends today.

Questioning her own sanity, Kate turned into the hardware store carpark in time to see three tails head down the side of the building. She pumped a fist in the air.

"They are here!" she yelled into her radio.

The dogs were there all right, but they were leaving.

"*This is unbelievable*," said Nelson, trusting his nose, but struggling to understand how Rex had figured it all out.

Rex said nothing in reply. They were close now, the dual scents hanging in the air more than enough to confirm the conclusion he drew back at the snack shack. The narrow passageway ran between the outer wall of the hardware store and the fence of the property next door – a wine wholesaler.

There was broken glass they needed to pick their way around and that slowed them down. However, despite the sense of urgency they felt, it was better than cutting their paws, and they could tell their target was stationary.

Coming around the side of the building, and peering through the fence into the hardware store's loading yard, Rex let a smile tease the corners of his mouth.

He didn't need to say anything; gloating about being right would just make him sound big headed.

Standing in the shade of the building, Anthony Stone was smoking a cigarette and sharing a joke with an overweight man. That the overweight man was the one from the snack shack was in no doubt in any one of the three dogs' minds – he stank of fish and grease. Nor did they question that the scent they found in abundance at the snack shack was that of the hardware store manager. The two men knew each other and to Rex that could only mean one thing – they were in it together.

When Rex and his fellow police dogs began barking, Kate and Harry sprinted to find them. Ruari was being too much of a grouch to follow, electing to wait by the vans because, "The stupid dog will just run away again anyway."

When they found them, the dogs had the store manager and another man cornered against the fence in the loading yard. The three dogs were positioned so they were fanned out to cut off any possible avenue of escape and contrary to their training, were just standing there, their lips pulled back to show their teeth, but not attacking.

"It was the strangest thing," Kate later explained to her husband at home. "That new dog knew. Don't ask me how, but he knew where to find the stolen gear and then he led us all the way back to the hardware store where the manager was getting his split of the cash that was stolen. He'd turned the cameras off and helped his accomplice to load a van with easily saleable tools and machines. Then he locked himself in the storeroom. Once we identified the other man as the bloke from the snack shack, they both confessed."

"What about the new fella?" Kate's husband enquired, trying to act like he was paying attention even though he was watching *Gold Seekers* on TV and really didn't care about Kate's miracle dog.

"He calmed down and agreed to keep working with Rex Harrison." Kate sucked some air between her teeth. "I don't see him lasting though."

"Which one?"

Kate scratched at an itch under her chin. "Either one of them. The dog might be the brightest one they ever trained, but if he can't obey his handler, he's not going to be a lot of use as a police dog."

Hellcat

Missing Rings

Albert frowned, his face creasing as he began poking about. Petunia's collection of engagement, wedding, and eternity rings were not where they always sat on her dressing table. They were there yesterday, weren't they? How could they go missing?

Rex wandered into his human's bedroom, wagging his tail lazily from side to side until he caught the scent of the cat. The unwelcome scent meant the cat had been in here again. He'd caught it sitting on his human's bed just yesterday, but this wasn't the lingering smell from then, this was fresh. He jumped up to put his front paws on the bed, sniffing along the cover to find the spot it had occupied.

'Down, Rex,' commanded his human, a kindly old man whose nose was just as unused as all others of his species. So far as Rex was concerned, humans were fun to be around, but also intensely frustrating as they ran around using their eyes and ears, when the information was right there if they would just sniff it in.

Albert stared at the dressing table again, moving things

around until he spotted the glint of gold. There they were, he signed with relief. His eldest grandson was planning to propose, he discovered yesterday. Martin was twenty-seven, a sensible age to be tying the knot, and though he hadn't been asked, Albert wanted to offer the ring he bought Petunia when he asked for her hand. It was a two-carat diamond with a cluster of lesser diamonds around it. It cost a silly amount at the time; three months wages, if his memory served him correctly, but she had been worth every hard-earned penny.

His frown returned: the engagement ring wasn't there. The eternity and wedding band were, but not the one he wanted. How had they come to move anyway? Turning to spy the dog, an oversized German Shepherd, who was now lifting the valance with his head as he looked under the bed, Albert said, 'Rex!' to get the dog's attention. He raised his voice to see if he could make the dog jump and chuckled when he heard the animal knock his head against the underside of the bed.

Rex popped back out, a scowl on his face. He played tricks on his human regularly - looking under things until his human gave in and got on the carpet to see what he was looking at was a favourite. He fell for it every time, even though there was never anything there to look at. However, it simply wasn't on for his human to get his own back.

'Rex, have you been in here messing with things?' asked Albert.

Rex raised one eyebrow. 'It was the cat. Can you seriously not smell it? It smells like evil mixed with gone-off fish.'

Albert stared down at the dog, wondering what the odd whining/chuffing noises were all about. 'Honestly, dog, I swear you are trying to answer me sometimes.'

Majestic Mystery

Rex walked up to the dressing table and gave it a sniff. Then made a surprised face because there was visible cat fur among the items displayed. Looking up at his human, Rex would have shaken his head if he knew to do so.

A knock at the door disturbed them and Rex exploded into action. He loved when people came to the door. It was the unexpected element that triggered his excitement. Behind the door could be anyone! It could be the postman with a parcel, or one of his human's children with his or her family; that was always fun. Or, it might be someone calling to see if Albert wanted to go to the pub. That happened sometimes. Forgetting the cat for a moment, Rex barked and ran, charging down the stairs to run at the door where he leapt up to place his front paws either side of the small frosted-glass window. A whiff of Old Spice cologne and moustache wax told him the person outside was the man from across the street.

Albert put the two rings into his trouser pocket as he made his way down to the front door. He had to fight Rex to get him out of the way, eventually shoving the daft dog back and holding his collar with one hand so he could open the door. The shadow outside proved to be Wing Commander Roy Hope, Albert's neighbour from across the road.

Albert wasn't expecting him, but the two men got on well and saw each other in church each week. Their wives had gone to school together and were friends their whole lives. Albert's wife, Petunia, had been gone for most of a year now, and the couple across the street liked to check in on him semi-regularly. Albert greeted his caller. 'Good morning, Roy.'

Roy wasn't one for chit chat, especially not when he had a purpose. 'I say, old boy, you've got a snooper.'

'A what?' said Albert, not sure he'd heard correctly.

'A snooper,' announced Roy again, speaking loudly as was his habit. However, he then leaned in close to whisper surreptitiously, 'It's that woman from number twenty-three. The odd-looking one who just moved in. She's up to something,' he concluded confidently.

Albert, a seventy-eight-year-old retired detective superintendent, was known by his children for poking his nose in when he thought a crime might be occurring, but he hadn't noticed anything untoward about the new neighbour two doors down. 'When you say snooping...' Albert prompted Roy for more.

Roy wriggled his upper lip, an act which made his pure-white bushy moustache dance about. 'She was looking through your windows, old boy. I saw her, blatant and bold as brass. Cupped her hands either side of her head and looked through your windows. Then she moved to a different spot. 'I dare say she was casing the joint and getting ready to burgle you.'

Albert almost snorted a laugh. The lady in question was in her mid-twenties and chose to dress in a manner which residents of the village might think unusual or odd, as Roy chose to put it. She was an EMO, Albert thought, though he struggled to keep up with all the fashions and trends now. Her clothing was mostly black and had a ravaged look to it. Apparently, it could be bought like that, even though, to Albert's mind, the wearer looked to have lost a fight with a tiger. The laugh which started to form, died when he remembered his wife's missing engagement ring. 'When was this?' he asked.

'Yesterday, old boy. And again this morning.'

Albert's eyebrows made a bid for freedom, hiking up his forehead as they tried to reach the summit of his scalp.

Majestic Mystery

Leaning from his door and craning his neck around to look in the direction of her house, he said, 'You say she was looking through my windows?' The comment was made more to himself than to Roy. 'I think I might need to find out who she is.'

Rex had been waiting patiently, but the scent of the cat was ripe on the air. Trained by the police to discern different smells, he'd qualified as a police dog only to be fired months later for having a bad attitude. The only dog in the history of the Metropolitan Police to ever get the sack, Rex had been loyal and obedient to his human handlers but despairing of their inability to use their olfactory systems to smell the clues. He generally worked out who the killer/robber/criminal was within minutes and got upset when the humans wouldn't listen to him.

The cat had been in his house, and Rex was going to have a word with it.

'Rex!' shouted Albert as his dog ran across the front lawn and leapt the low hedge into his neighbour's garden.

'Won't be a minute!' barked Rex.

'What's got him so excited?' asked Roy.

Albert muttered some expletives, ducking back into his house to snag the dog lead from its hook. Then, when Rex stopped at number twenty-three and started sniffing around the house, he saw an opportunity.

'It would appear that I need to retrieve my dog,' he announced as if orating to the back row of a theatre. He'd spotted something of interest already and had a legitimate reason to take a closer look.

'You're going over there, old boy?' Roy wiggled his moustache, and set off too, ambling down the street with a sense of righteous purpose.

Rex would go into the house to find the cat if someone

would open the door, but he could smell that the cat had been through the overgrown undergrowth at the front of the house in the last few minutes. That meant it might still be outside. He followed the smell to the side of the house where a tall wrought iron gate barred his progress.

He could hear his human calling his name. A quick glance over his shoulder revealed the old man and his friend with the facial hair coming to him. Heaven's be praised, they understood for once: the cat needed to be taught a lesson.

He pawed the gate, making it clang as it moved, but it wouldn't open. Frustrated, Rex peered into the dark space down the side of the house where the gate led to a path overgrown with more weeds and shaded by an out-of-control wisteria. The scent of the cat was rife now, though Rex couldn't believe it when the evil feline wandered into view.

Rex barked his displeasure. The cat sat on its haunches and began to lazily lick a front paw. This was the first time Rex had seen it. Until now, all he got was the smell to let him know it had been in his garden and into his house, finding itself a comfortable place to sleep on his human's bed – a place where Rex wasn't allowed to go! The cat was missing its left eye, which gave it a hellish appearance when combined with the tattered left ear. Then Rex noticed the stumpy tail when the cat flicked it in an annoyed way.

Rex barked again, louder this time, letting the cat know what was in store if Rex caught it on his land again. The cat flicked its tail and sauntered away in an overly casual manner.

Albert and Roy arrived at the front of the property, opening the garden gate to proceed down the path to the door.

Seeing them, Rex barked, crouching his front end, and signalling as the police handlers had taught him. 'It's right down here! Open the gate and I'll get it!' Rex knocked the gate again with his skull, keen to get through it and teach the cat a swift lesson in humility.

From his front door, Albert could see an envelope dangling from the letterbox. Rex's decision to go to the property gave him a perfect reason to see if the homeowner's name was on it.

'Why is he barking madly like that?' asked Roy. He couldn't see anything that would make the dog want to continue to bark.

Roy's question gave Albert pause, his dismissive answer about the dog being bonkers dying on his lips as he observed Rex's behaviour. Was he alerting? That's what it looked like. He knew Rex's background as a police dog. Albert's three children were all serving senior police officers; a call to his youngest one was all it took to scoop one of many dogs who failed the training. He only found out afterwards that he'd been duped and given a problem dog who passed the training but then couldn't be managed.

Whatever the case, Rex was displaying behaviour he'd seen before in other police dogs. If he were interpreting it correctly, his dog could smell one of three things: drugs, guns, or cash. 'Rex, to me,' he used his insistent voice and the dog complied.

'It's back there somewhere,' Rex whined. 'I'm not going to hurt it. I just want to make sure it doesn't come into the house again.'

To Roy, Albert murmured, 'I need to make a phone call.'

Professional Busybody

Albert stayed in his neighbour's front garden confident his dog had made so much noise that there couldn't be anyone home. Yet if someone did come to the door, Albert had a line prepared in his head about wanting to welcome their new neighbour in person. He plucked the envelope from the letterbox, fishing for his reading glasses only to discover he'd left them at home

Albert offered the letter to Roy with his left hand, using his right to dig around for his phone. 'Can you read this and tell me what name is on the address?'

Thinking it likely the letter was for the previous resident since the new owner only just moved in, Albert was pleased when Roy said, 'Ophelia James.' The person in the house previously was Darren somethingorother.

The ringing in his ear stopped when his call was answered, the voice of his youngest son echoing loud and clear. 'Hello, Dad.'

'Are you at work?' Albert asked, getting straight to the point – a trait he'd instilled in his children at an early age.

At the other end of the call, Chief Inspector Randall Smith pursed his lips. His dad didn't call very often, and when he did, it tended to be because he wanted to know something he couldn't find out for himself. 'I am,' Randall replied cautiously.

'Super.' Albert grinned at Roy and waggled his eyebrows. 'Can you look up the name Ophelia James for me, please, son?'

Randall sighed. As he suspected, his father was poking his nose into someone's business. It wasn't the first time, it wouldn't be the last, but helping him with information generally resulted in trouble. 'I don't think I should do that, dad.'

Albert's smile froze. 'Why ever not? I think I'm onto something, Randall.'

'Like the time you thought the verger was sending poison pen letters?' Randall reminded him.

'He *was* sending them!' snapped Albert. 'He got arrested for it last week.'

This was news to Randall, not that he expected to hear of every crime committed in his home county; he worked in London after all. Nevertheless, he narrowed his eyes and questioned his father. 'Are you making that up, dad?'

'No! Patricia Fisher caught him. She's got quite the nose for solving crime, that one. She should have gone into the police herself.'

Dismissing that line of conversation, Randall said, 'Who is Ophelia James and what is it that you think she might have done?'

Albert thought about how to answer Randall's question in such a way that his son would relent and use his computer to provide the information he wanted. He couldn't think of anything though, so he just said, 'She's been looking through my windows and your mother's engagement ring is missing. Also, Rex is alerting at her house so there might be drugs here. Or a body,' Albert added quickly, thinking it might prompt his son to comply. 'There's definitely something going on and I just want you to check to see if she has a record.'

'I'm sorry, Dad. I have an insurance scam case I need to crack. All my time has to be devoted to that.'

'Insurance scam you say?' Albert feigned interest, hoping to keep his son talking long enough to change his mind.

Randall groaned. 'Yes, Dad. A person gets a call from a firm who sound real, has a website, and are offering a great introductory rate. They target older people a lot; it's all very ugly and they can get away with people's life savings. Anyway, there's a new crew operating in this area and I'm getting a lot of pressure to catch them. If you don't mind, Dad, I really need to get back to the investigation I am supposed to be leading.'

Albert could sense that further persistence would lead to an argument and he remembered being under pressure to produce a result. To end the call, he said, 'Very good, Randall. I'm sure you'll get them.'

Roy, who hadn't heard the other half of the conversation, asked, 'We are on our own?'

'Very much,' Albert grumbled. Skewing his lips to one side, he fished the rings from his pocket to show Roy. 'My Petunia's engagement ring is missing. Quite inexplicably missing,' he added. 'It was there the last time I looked, which might have been yesterday, but someone had disturbed the things on her dressing table, and they took her diamond engagement ring. I was planning to give it to my grandson if he wanted it.'

Roy narrowed his eyes at Mrs James's front door. 'And this woman has been snooping at your windows, old boy. I dare say there's a connection.'

Rex listened to the exchange, pointing out each time either human paused that it was the cat they needed to speak to. They just weren't listening, a human trait which had always irked him. The cat was here somewhere, possibly inside the house if the back door was open or it had one of those cat flap thingies.

He chose to investigate again since the humans were just standing around talking.

Albert was faced with a dilemma. Law abiding his entire life - he had to be, of course, but his wife's ring was missing, and this woman had been looking through his windows. He reached a decision, stepping forward to rap his knuckles smartly on the doorframe.

'You going to confront her, old boy?' asked Roy, somewhat surprised by the escalation.

Albert turned his head to the side and spoke over his shoulder, 'I'm going to introduce myself and ask if there was something she wanted. I can make out like I saw her outside my house. I'll be the friendly neighbour, and we shall see how she responds. You can tell if a person is lying by what their eyes do,' he told Roy knowingly.

He didn't get to check out her eyes though because no one came to the door. He chose to try again, opting to use the heavy brass knocker on the door this time. However, when he lifted it, the door moved: it wasn't closed, only pushed to. With the slightest tap of his index finger, the door moved two inches.

Rex got no luck at the side of the house, the cat hadn't returned to taunt him from behind the gate, but when he looked back at the two humans, he saw they had the front door open. Rex had never really understood the concept of property: if he peed on it, it was his. Wasn't that a simpler solution? Humans had all manner of strange rules about who could go where. Rex chose to ignore them because they made no sense, saw the chance to get his own back on the cat by invading the cat's place which he intended to mark as his own once inside, and ran for the widening gap.

Albert never saw him coming, the dog streaking past his legs to fly inside the house. 'Rex, no!' he yelled, which had as much effect as throwing a spider web in front of a charging bull.

'I know you're in here, cat!' barked Rex. 'Let's see how you like it! Where's your favourite spot? I'll be sure to mark that one!'

His human was shouting something discouraging - he often did. Rex, however, knew it was his job to keep the cat out of his human's house and that was what he was going to do.

Dumbfounded on the doorstep, Albert grimaced at his friend the wing commander. 'I've got to go after him. Heaven knows what damage he might do. The poor woman hasn't even had a chance to settle in yet.'

'It doesn't look like she's unpacked,' observed Roy, peering through the now wide-open door at the boxes stacked against the walls.

From inside, they could hear Rex barking. Then a thump as the dog knocked something over. Albert swore and went into the house. He knew that by law he wasn't technically breaking and entering. He didn't have the homeowner's permission, but the door was unlocked, and he would be able to argue that he felt it necessary to retrieve his dog. Another crashing noise propelled him across the threshold just in time to hear the squeal of a cat as it screeched somewhere deeper in the house.

'Should we be in here, old boy?' asked Roy, joining Albert inside the house.

Rex was barking insanely now, toward the back of the house and loud enough to alert people in the next village. The cat was spitting and hissing in return with just as much volume. Albert expected to find the cat backed into a space too small for his dumb, oversized German Shepherd to penetrate, but he didn't get the chance to find out because the next thump was followed instantly by the sound of scrambling feet as the cat ran and the dog chased.

Albert and Roy were in the narrow hallway that ran alongside the stairs when the cat rounded the corner ahead of them, leaning into the bend and running for all it was worth. It's much lower centre of gravity ensured it could turn quicker than the dog, which appeared about a heartbeat later, slamming into the wall opposite the room he was leaving because he was moving altogether too fast to change direction.

Rex struck the wood panelling with a jarring blow to his right shoulder, but it wasn't going to slow him down for long. The cat had said several unkind things about his mother and the local stray dogs – it was not the sort of thing he could forgive, not on top of the blatant home invasion. The cat had earned itself a chewed tail at the very least.

Bouncing off the wall, Rex put his head down and powered on. The cat was going to go out of the front door, he could see the opening ahead of him, daylight streaming in enticingly. Once the cat was out in the open, he would be able to catch him.

Albert's eyes flared as the cat shot between his feet and

the dog looked set to follow. Mercifully, Rex made himself thin, squeezing against the wall to pass by his human's legs without touching them.

'Don't worry!' barked Rex. 'I'll get him when he goes outside!'

But the cat didn't go outside, he banked hard at the bottom of the stairs and flew up them. Rex's paws slipped and slid over the hallway carpet as he tried to follow. His butt slammed against the front door, banging it back against the wall as he finally got his legs under control.

'Rex!' Albert bellowed after the dog, but Rex was already powering up the stairs when Albert shouted, 'Leave the cat alone!'

Rex didn't slow down but he did hear what his human said. It mystified him. Why were they here if it wasn't to deal with the cat? He got to the landing and had a choice of directions. The house smelled of the cat; enough so that he was finding it difficult to determine which way the cat went. Huffing in frustration, he put his nose to the carpet and started sniffing his way along.

Albert called again, yelling the dog's name to no avail. 'I'd better go after him,' he grumbled, placing his hand on the banister.

Wondering what he ought to do and feeling like an unnecessary extra because he wasn't adding any value, Roy volunteered, 'I'll come with you. Many hands and all that.'

Both pensioners made their way up the stairs using the handrail to give them a bit of extra oomph, but just as they reached the landing and both turned right toward the front of the house, the cat shot out of a bedroom behind them and bolted back down the stairs.

Rex was hot on the cat's heels and, to Albert, it looked

as if he'd managed to nip the cat's backend or tail because he had bits of fur stuck to his jowls.

Now sensing victory, Rex took the stairs in two bounds, his powerful legs driving him on at a pace the cat couldn't match. The cat's only chance was to climb, but there were no trees outside. Rex wasn't going to hurt it, he just wanted to establish some ground rules. It was bad enough that he had to share his garden with the local squirrel mafia, but a cat that believed it could come into his house and sit on his human's bed? Well, there were limits to what he would tolerate. It didn't help that the cat looked like something the devil might have vomited.

However, going as fast as possible proved to be a mistake. At the bottom of the stairs, he had altogether too much momentum to switch from a downward trajectory to a horizontal one. He crashed into the carpet, knocked into a coatrack, and slammed the door back against its stops. The cat was gone, haring across the front lawn by the time Rex looked up. Only a heartbeat had passed but the front door was swinging shut.

Snarling at his choice of pace over planning, Rex bounced back onto his feet and shot through the gap before the door slammed shut behind him with a thump.

At the top of the stairs, Albert swore yet again. The dog was finally out of the house, but the stupid beast didn't have the sense to stay where he could be found. He might chase the cat to the next county before it occurred to him to question where he was.

'Do you think we should look for Petunia's ring?' asked Roy. When Albert turned to look at him questioningly, he added, 'Since we are already here.'

It was a tempting proposition, but not a sensible one. 'We should go. The lady was snooping through my windows, that doesn't mean she came inside. It doesn't mean she did anything wrong at all. This is her house, and we shouldn't be in it.'

Roy nodded, knowing his friend was right, and they made toward the stairs.

With his foot poised to descend the first step, he heard the distinctive sound of a car pulling onto the driveway.

Trapped/Ambush

Rex leapt the fence that bordered the front of the garden, following the cat. 'I'm gonna get you, cat!' he barked as he chased after it, his tongue lolling from the right side of his mouth. He'd heard the shouts from his human - it wasn't so much that he chose to ignore him, Rex simply knew what was best. If his human's nose worked properly, he would know the cat had been in the bedroom and would be thanking Rex for his diligence.

The cat shot under a car, evading Rex just when he was almost close enough to pounce. Forced to stop and go around, Rex lost sight of the cat and had to use his nose to continue the chase. Down a side alley between the houses, Rex plunged through brambles and gnarly undergrowth that pulled at his fur. He barely noticed any of it because the cat had somehow given him the slip. Had it found a bolt hole in the mouth of the alley and slipped through it to escape?

He would have to go back and check, but he pushed on another yard first because a leafy green bush obscured what was ahead and the whole area stunk of cat. Bursting through the bush, leaves exploding in every direction, Rex skidded to a stop. It was a blind alley and he'd reached the end. He spun around to go back but, confronted with an unexpected sight, he froze to the spot in shock. Now he understood why the alleyway smelled of cats.

Back at the house, Albert and Roy were also frozen to the spot. Below them, the front door swung open - Ophelia was back from wherever she had gone, and they were intruders in her house. How could they possibly talk their way out of this one? It wasn't as if the story about the dog would work any longer, Rex was goodness knows where by now, probably still chasing the cat.

Albert felt a pang of concern for his big, dopey dog, but he had a bigger problem right now: what to do? The sensible thing would be to call out to Ophelia, give her a completely honest explanation and beg for her forgiveness. She could call the police, and if she did, he would wait patiently for their arrival. Embarrassment was the biggest issue.

Roy whispered, 'Any thoughts, old boy? We seem to have landed ourselves in a bit of a pickle.'

Unwilling to speak because he could see Ophelia from his position at the top of the stairs. She was standing in the hallway, taking off her boots, bending over awkwardly to unzip them one at a time with her left hand. Her right hand was holding her phone to her ear. Employing a professional voice, she sounded like she was selling someone a life insurance policy or something similar. Too engrossed in her work, she didn't see the two old men standing at the top of the stairs. While they gawped at her and wondered what to do, she padded out of sight through her house in stockinged feet.

If they were quick (and lucky) they might be able to slip out undetected!

'That's our gold star, award-winning policy,' Albert heard Ophelia say as he carefully placed his right foot on the next step down. 'Yes, Mrs Hatton, that will cover all your funeral expenses and leave a very worthwhile cash sum behind.' There was a pause while the person at the other end spoke; Mrs Hatton's voice impossible to hear, of course. 'Yes, we can set that up right now, Mrs Hatton. All it will take is an initial credit card payment of fifty pounds. That verifies the account and the money will be transferred to your investment pot so you're not really paying anything, you're just investing it.'

Albert listened intently for just a few seconds. He was trying to work out how to announce his presence without causing the poor woman to wet herself with fright. But as the conversation went on, he began to wonder what he was listening to. Ophelia James sounded as if she were working for a big insurance firm, but Albert had never heard of Silver Linings Life Insurance and Bond. Not that his knowledge extended to encompass every firm on the planet, but to his detective's brain, there was something fishy going on.

Roy tapped Albert on the shoulder, startling him to the point that he almost had a south of the border accident. While his heart restarted, and Roy whispered an apology, the conversation downstairs shifted gear: Mrs Hatton was ready to make her initial deposit and Ophelia was coming their way!

'Yes, Mrs Hatton. Customers who deposit over two hundred pounds when they open their account do obtain access to a higher level of interest. The ladder system Silver Linings employ has a top tier of four percent net interest for those customers able to deposit an initial sum of a thousand pounds.' She was coming back along the hall and there was nothing that way except the front door and the stairs.

Albert backed into Roy, bumping into him where he frantically gesticulated that he should turn around and start moving. 'Hide!' Albert whispered, giving his friend a shove to get him moving. There were three bedrooms and a bathroom to pick from and no way of knowing which direction might be the safe one. They turned left, toward the back of the house, their shuffling tiptoe steps carrying them swiftly into a small bedroom filled with nothing but unopened boxes.

They heard Ophelia jog up the stairs, her younger legs making a mockery of the effort it took them, but as they held their breath, uncertain where she might be heading, they heard her turn right toward the front of the house.

Peeking through a gap between the door and its frame, Albert could see her swift movements. The phone was cradled between shoulder and ear to give her two free hands. Diagonally across the corridor, he could see her frantically moving items around to uncover what she wanted: a laptop computer.

'Yes, Mrs Hatton. I can take the deposit now. You wish to take advantage of our one time only joining bonus? I must congratulate you on your vision, Mrs Hatton. You have invested wisely.' There came a brief pause while Mrs Hatton spoke, then Ophelia said, 'I just need to take the long number from your credit card.' Sixty seconds later, the call ended with a whoop as Ophelia celebrated her sale.

Albert was already more than a little suspicious, but her next words left him with no doubt.

'Another sucker,' she cheered. 'There's one born every minute.' Ophelia was scamming people, selling them a fake insurance policy, and taking their money. Her victims would never get anything for their investment and her number was most likely blocked so once the call ended their money had already been paid into her account and there was no way to get it back. There would be layers of confusion hiding the money as it transferred from one account to another, but even if the victim were to report the fraud, they willingly paid the money and who is to say what conversation had taken place after the fact.

This type of fraud was in its infancy when Albert retired from the police, and he worked murder investigations more regularly. Today he knew there were teams of boffins set up to track down criminals involved in internet and phone-based fraud. Computer forensics they called it. His kids talked about it sometimes.

The question at the front of Albert's brain now, was what to do about it?

Across the street in the alleyway between the houses, Rex found himself surrounded.

He'd run blindly into the alley, assured of his dominance and supremacy. However, the confident feeling, crashing through the undergrowth using sheer power and determination to force his way through, now seeped away as four dozen sets of eyes stared back at him.

The cat he'd been chasing stood front and centre where it meowelled at him, a deep, evil noise that spoke of violence and spitefully sharp claws. A ball of worry found its way to the pit of his stomach as yet more cats pushed their way through the undergrowth or walked along the top edge of the fence six feet above the ground.

He tried a defiant bark, 'Oh yeah, kitty cats!' Even he could hear that it sounded forced though. He backed away a pace, only to hear another cat emit its low mournful growl from the wall that blocked off the alley.

Now scared for his exposed backend, Rex started to look for a way out.

The cats were edging closer, their tails bolt upright and the fur spread out to make them look like bottle brushes. Coming in on all sides and from above, there wasn't a single direction he could go that appeared to be safe.

Seeing no choice, he bunched his muscles.

Confession Time

'Randall, it's Dad,' Albert whispered into his phone.

Randall slumped his head onto his free hand. He was getting nowhere with the stupid insurance scam case and his dad wouldn't leave him alone. He accepted that he wasn't the best-behaved child growing up, but he was forty-one and surely his past crimes ought to be forgiven by now. Why was his father continuing to punish him?

'Why are you whispering, Dad?' he asked.

Albert didn't answer immediately. The sound of Ophelia moving around downstairs had stopped, like she thought she heard something and froze her body to listen more intently. When he heard her flick the kettle on, he let go the breath he held and continued to whisper, 'Son, I've got a confession to make which you won't like, but I also think I might have found your insurance scammer. Or one of them at least.'

Randall jerked forward in his chair, excited for a second, but then, analysing what his father just said, he closed his eyes to ask, 'What is the confession, Dad?'

Albert considered how to broach the subject but decided there really wasn't a good way to admit he was guilty of trespass.

'Dad?' prompted Randall, still waiting for the confession to come.

'Okay, Randall, here it is. You need to come to number twenty-three Hibiscus Drive. The woman I asked you about earlier - Ophelia James? Well she is involved in the insurance fraud you are investigating. Or she is involved in a separate insurance scam, but either way, you need to seize her laptop and have your forensic computer boffins go over it. It's in her front bedroom.'

Randall's deep frown deepened yet further, creasing his forehead to bring his hairline almost down to the point where it touched his eyebrows. 'How do you know ... hold on, are you in her house?' The idea that his elderly father might misbehave that badly horrified him, but he already felt certain it was true.

'Of course not, son,' Albert lied. 'I'll explain when you get here. You probably ought to bring a crime scene van.'

Randall wanted his father's claims to be true. The computer and phone fraud people were so elusive. Catching them always took months of painstaking hard work and then they had to prove, without question, the person's criminal intentions only to find, all too often, it was the minnow they had snared, not the big fish running it. Nevertheless, he knew he had to at least check out his father's claim. He was due to brief the chief constable at five o'clock and it would be nice to have something to tell him for once.

With a huff of exhalation from his nose, Randall, pushed back his chair and started to get up. 'All right, Dad. I'll be there shortly. If you are in her house ...'

'I'm not, son,' Albert lied again. Roy tugged on Albert's

shirt, trying to get his attention. Albert lifted a finger to beg a moment's grace.

'Just don't be by the time I get there, okay?' warned Randall.

'We'll meet you outside.' Albert promised, hoping he could find a way to make that true. Roy was tugging on his shirt again, so he ended the call quickly by adding, 'See you soon.' Putting his phone away, he turned to see what Roy wanted so urgently and felt the blood drain from his face.

Ophelia was standing in the doorway to the back bedroom, holding a small calibre handgun on them. Cocking her head to one side, she snarled, 'Who the heck are you two?'

Hell Cat

The cat had lured him into a blind alley and the only way out was through the platoon of feline horrors facing him. Rex leapt as the cats came for him. His powerful jaws were no match for hundreds of tiny, razor sharp claws and he knew it. His only way to minimise injury was to put his head down and run, so that was what he did.

In the house, Ophelia took a step back, leaving the doorway as she moved into the upper hallway. Her gun never wavered, pointing directly at the two men. With her left hand, she reached into the back pocket of her jeans, producing a phone. She didn't speak to Albert and Roy as she lifted it to her ear.

'Donny? Yeah, I've got intruders in my house. I think they know about the scam.' She turned her head away slightly, grimacing at whatever Donny said in reply. 'I don't know, do I? I just heard them upstairs in my house. No, the new house.' Clearly Donny was displeased with what she had to tell him. 'Look, they need to be disposed of. Just get over here.'

The call ended with a note of finality and she backed up further to the stairs. 'Come along, old codgers. You picked the wrong house to snoop today.'

'Why were you snooping at my house?' asked Albert, thinking it was a good idea to keep her talking.

Her brow furrowed. 'Your house. I have no idea who you are, old man.'

'I live at number nineteen. My name is Albert Smith and I have already called the police. They are on their way here now.'

Ophelia snorted a laugh. 'Nice try, old man. Even if the heat do show up, you won't be here and there's nothing in the house to prove I've done anything wrong. Donny's system is perfect: no overhead, isolated units working alone, undetectable. Much better than any of the other scams I've worked. Now, move!' she jerked the gun at them, beckoning they both follow.

Albert didn't want to, but he saw little option, and they couldn't hope to escape from upstairs, so they needed to go down anyway. With their hands aloft, Albert, then Roy, followed her down the stairs. Ophelia walked backwards, but the faint hope Albert held that she might trip and fall, came to naught.

Donny, it seemed, lived close by, for the call was only two minutes old when a van pulled up outside. 'You see?' smiled Ophelia, 'You'll be long gone before the police can show up. You're going for a nice drive in the countryside.'

The door opened to reveal a large man with a crew cut. He had a bullet shaped head which was tattooed to create a mask of sorts on his face and he had multiple piercings which distorted his nose, lips, and ears. His outfit, if one could even call it that, made him look like an Ewok who had been attacked with a hedge-trimmer.

Donny's face curled into an unpleasant sneer. 'Who are these two?' he growled.

Her gun still pinning both men in place, Ophelia replied, 'My neighbours, I think. That one,' she jerked the gun at Albert, 'Says I was looking through his window earlier.'

'Were you?' asked Donny.

'I was looking for my cat.'

'That flea-bitten thing is still alive?' he growled.

'You leave Hellcat alone,' she frowned. 'He and I have been through a lot together. He's just settling into a new place, that's all. He likes to explore other people's houses.'

'Yeah, whatever,' Donny shut off the conversation. 'The van's outside, and there's no one around.' He looked directly at Albert and Roy. 'I'll have to gag and tie them. I've got some carpet in the van to roll them in. They can go into Cliffe Lake. It'll be a few centuries before anyone finds them.'

Albert couldn't stop himself from gulping at the calm manner in which Donny discussed their dispatch. Behind him, Roy was fiddling with his walking cane. A nervous habit, Albert was sure.

Donny opened the front door to get the things from his van, but as he took a step forward, a blur of something brown hit his shins.

With a girlish squeal of shock, Donny flew into the air, but the blur wasn't done yet. Unable to slow down, it piled through Ophelia who was facing Albert and never even saw it coming. She too went from perpendicular to horizontal in the blink of an eye, crashing back to the hallway carpet in a confusion of limbs and a cry of pain.

Albert was fast to seize the slim chance they'd been

given, kicking the gun from Ophelia's hand where it skittered free to hit the skirting board.

Roy went around Albert's back, a glint of reflected sunlight drawing Albert's eye to the thin sword the wing commander had drawn from his walking cane. His eyes went wide, but not as wide as Donny's who found the tip of the sword skewering the front of his shirt.

Like an old, yet still dashing Robin Hood, Roy barked, 'I may be getting on, young man, but I'm willing to bet my sword can find your heart before you can draw your next breath. I suggest you lie still.'

Bewildered by the turn of events, Albert looked at Rex. His dog was panting hard and he had blood dripping from half a dozen different facial cuts. With a finger pointed at Ophelia, Albert commanded, 'Rex, guard!' the dog instantly curled his top lip and growled at the woman who stank of the cat.

Outside the door, a flash of red and blue caught his attention: Randall was here, his son's disbelieving face framed in the side window of his car.

Aftermath

The sun was beginning to set when Roy's wife wandered across with his evening glass of port. She brought one for Albert too, the men clinking their small glasses together in a toast.

They were sitting on two fold-out garden chairs, also provided by Mrs Hope. Rex's wounds proved to be superficial, tiny slices in his nose, eyebrows, and ears but the combined effect made it look like he'd run though a reel of razor wire.

Randall emerged from the house, shaking his head in disbelief. 'We've got it all, Dad. The contacts on their phones have led us to the other scammers in the ring. They are all being arrested as we speak. The chief constable is over the moon.'

Donny and Ophelia had been arrested and taken away already, both protesting their innocence but with evidence stacked against them. Albert didn't think they would see freedom for a while. Her possession of a firearm and the likelihood that Donny's van had been used to transport other captive persons, would carry more weight than the fraud charges anyway.

Randall checked around to make sure no one was within earshot before lowering his voice to say, 'I just have one question, Dad. Why were you anywhere near her house?'

The sound of a cat hacking loudly stopped Albert from answering straight away, but it was his giant fearless dog backing away that made him pay attention to it. The cat was Ophelia's, they discovered. When it appeared earlier, she begged the police to look after it. They were waiting for the RSPCA to arrive because it looked like it needed urgent veterinary treatment, or perhaps euthanasia. Right now, it was hunched over, it's mouth open as it heaved a giant hairball onto the lawn.

Disgusted, but unable to look away, Albert, Roy, and Randall all saw the glint of something shiny ooze out of the slimy mess. It finally broke free of the gunk, plopping to the ground where it rolled over.

Randall moved closer, the cat opting to scurry away with a hiss. 'It's a ring,' he observed.

Rex laid down with a huff and put his head on his front paws. 'I told you it was the cat,' he sighed.

The Case of the Missing Pasty

Immediate Cessation of Biscuit Ration

Albert stared at the crumbs that represented what remained of his lunch, a deep frown forming on his brow. The crumbs didn't bother him so much; it was the fact that he hadn't eaten the delicious, warm Cornish pasty fresh from the bakers that irked.

"Rex!" Albert raised his voice so the dog would hear. When no sound of movement returned, Albert used a single fingernail to tap on Rex's biscuit tin. "Oh, Rex," he called again, this time in an inviting sing-song voice.

Dozing in a sunbeam coming through the living room window, Rex heard his human when he shouted, but saw no need to react. However, the unmistakable sound of the old man touching his biscuit tin was enough to get him moving.

Arriving on the kitchen tile with a skid, Rex was surprised to see his biscuit tin mysteriously sitting on the shelf in its usual spot. High above his head, Rex knew only too well why it was there – the delicious, crunchy treats were far too tempting to resist. Were the tin to be left within biting range, as it had been on more than on occasion (this was biscuit tin number four) he would gorge himself on the contents.

"Biscuit?" Rex asked, tilting his head to one side as he tried to decipher why his human had his hands balled on his hips and a stern expression on his face.

Albert swivelled to one side, revealing the empty plate on the kitchen counter. With the flourish of an arm, wafted at the forlorn item of crockery, Albert said, "Well?"

Rex tilted his head again. The old man was upset about something, however the why of it remained a mystery. Following the arm, he padded across the room until his nose was beneath the plate.

With a deep sniff to confirm what he already knew, Rex said, "Cornish pasty from Capons in the High Street. A fine selection. Was it good?" Rex was being polite because his human was acting out of sorts. He loved the old man, but like all humans, his behaviour defied explanation most of the time.

What Rex really wanted to ask was why Alert hadn't bought two.

Albert heard the dog's grunting/huffing noises and as usual misinterpreted them.

"Tasty, was it?" he asked.

Rex twisted his head around to look up at the old man's face.

"Huh?" Unlike Albert, Rex had little trouble figuring out what his human meant. "I didn't eat it. I thought you did." That his human had not, in fact, ingested the meaty pastry treat was patently clear, yet it also generated a few questions, the chief among which was: if Albert didn't eat it, and I didn't eat it, then who did?

"This is not what I expect, Rex," Albert employed his disappointed voice. "You're not a puppy and you are not hungry. You had a perfectly good breakfast not more than a few hours ago. You even ate the paper bag the pasty came in," he added, Albert's frown deepening further as he wondered what that might do his dog's inner workings.

It wasn't in his nature to raise a hand – he never had with any of his children, and his relationship with the dog was just as deep though in a very different way. Rex was more of a pal than a dependent. The two had been through some adventures together and Albert knew for a fact that he wouldn't be alive now were it not for the dog saving his life more than once.

Huffing out a breath of acceptance that ruffled his lips, Albert patted Rex on the head.

"Go back to your sunspot while I find myself something else for lunch. You're on a biscuit ban for the next few days."

Rex's eyebrows reached for the sky. "But I didn't eat the pasty! What the heck is this? You used to be a police detective," he pointed out. "What happened to innocent until proven guilty?"

Albert was already peering into the refrigerator, skewing his face to one side as he pondered his options. Despite the months travelling the British Isles supposedly learning to cook for himself, he was still mostly hopeless when it came to anything more complex than a sandwich.

He'd tried. He'd even bought a pork pie dolly and all the ingredients to make his own batch of hand raised savoury pies, but the net result was inedible. He just didn't possess the finesse required for making his own treats, and had resorted to visiting the local high-end supermarket where he could find most of what he wanted.

Grumping and groaning loud enough to ensure Rex

heard it, Albert took out cheese, ham, pickled onions, and butter. A sandwich was a fine thing if crafted with care.

Annoyed that he was being blamed, and disappointed that he hadn't eaten the pasty since he was being punished for it, Rex decided he was going to find the culprit and clear his name.

Repeat Offender

Angus, the West Highland Terrier next door listened with great interest as Rex tried to explain the smell.

"It was faint, but it was right there near to where the pasty had been. There's no way I'm wrong."

"But not a cat," Angus wanted to confirm. Rex twitched one eyebrow, looking down at his neighbour with a look that suggested the terrier needed to stop asking stupid questions. "No. Right," said Angus, seeing the look he was getting. "If it was a cat, we wouldn't be talking about it."

"No," agreed Rex. "Even if it was a new cat, it would be easy to identify. This is something else and whatever it is, it's not something I have ever smelled before."

Dmitry appeared, the Great Dane from the house on the other side of Angus landing his paws atop the garden fence when he jumped up to look over.

"Did I just hear you discussing a mysterious break in?" Dmitry asked.

"Sure did," yipped Angus. "Rex has a strange smell in his kitchen and a missing pasty."

"From Capons on the High Street?" Dmitry asked, his mouth starting to salivate.

Rex rolled his eyes. The origin of the missing pasty was hardly important. To move things along he said, "Yes. I got blamed for eating it, and now I'd like to know who did."

Dmitry said, "There's a fresh Capons bag in my garden and it stinks of pasty." The statement jolted Rex into paying attention. "And a sandwich went missing from Henry's lunchbox yesterday while my human was making it." It left behind a strange smell: animal, but not something I've ever smelled before. I got blamed for taking it," Dmitry lamented. "Which is ridiculous because I would have taken the entire contents of the lunch box, not one sandwich."

Now this *was* news. They had a repeat thief. An opportunistic pilferer who was sneaking into houses to steal food from under their noses. How was it that none of them knew what it was?

Angus had a question that had been bothering him for a couple of days. "Do you think it might be the same animal that shredded my humans' rubbish bags?"

"It wasn't cats?" asked Rex, falling into the same trap Angus had a few minutes ago. "Nevermind," he got in before anyone else could speak. "Forget I asked."

Angus replied anyway. "Cats had been in it, but I don't think they were the ones who opened the bags."

Dmitry asked, "Why not?"

Angus had to think about that. "The claw marks were different for a start. It was the smell though. It was very … not catty," he struggled to find a description that fit.

"Monkey?" suggested Dmitry.

Rex stared at the Great Dane.

"We live in the southeast of England," Rex pointed out. "It's not known for its monkey population."

"Squirrel then," Dmitry fired back a little huffily.

Rex snapped out his response, "We know what squirrels smell like." Rex was becoming inpatient with the 'help' he was getting. It was his biscuit ration at stake for heaven's sake. Didn't the other dogs understand the stress he was under?

"Aardvark then," growled Dmitry, not used to being snarled at.

This time Rex had no reply accept to ask, "What the heck is an aardvark?" He checked with the West Highland Terrier to see if he was being dense.

Angus gave Rex the canine equivalent of a shrug. "Beats me," Angus said, turning around to join Rex in hitting Dmitry with a quizzical look.

Dmitry scowled at his neighbours for a minute, but couldn't maintain it. With a snort of laughter, he admitted, "I haven't the faintest idea. My human's child has a cuddly toy one that he carries everywhere. All I know is it's a strange looking thing with a long nose."

"How long?" asked Angus.

Rex felt like dropping a rock on the terrier's head. "The aadvark's nose is not important," he insisted, closing his eyes and wishing he'd never started the conversation. "My biscuits are. We have an intruder. The same one appears to have targeted all three of our properties. Do you know what that tells us?" He made eye contact with Dmitry and then Angus, encouraging them to see the obvious.

Angus yipped, "It can pick locks!" Then with a gasp of sudden realisation that made the small dog's eyes widen, he added, "It's got keys for fingers!"

"What? No," Rex couldn't figure out where that answer had come from.

"It's a master villain cat who can disguise it's smell and

has an imp or a pixie in its employment," volunteered Dmitry. "The cat was wronged by one of us many years ago and now it has returned to seek revenge." He delivered the concept in a staged voice to which he gave an eerie, sinister edge.

"Have you been drinking?" asked Rex. "An imp or a pixie?"

Dmitry tried to defend his suggestion. "Janice two down from me says she has pixies in her garden. They play in the sun, but always vanish when she tries to catch them. She can hear them whispering though, even when she can't see them."

Rex just wanted to figure out who stole his human's pasty and had thought it might not be a terrible idea to include a few of his neighbours in the investigation – three noses are better than one. Now he was wondering what he done to deserve being shackled with these two nitwits.

Speaking slowly, he pointed out, "For starters, Janice is a cat, Dmitry. Every other word leaving her mouth is a lie. Plus, everyone knows Janice knows where her human keeps the catnip supply. She's stoned ninety-five percent of the time. What having the same thief coming in to all our houses means," he got in quick before either dog could offer another stupid reply, "is that the thief is local."

"Ohhhh, yeahhh," drawled Dmitry and Angus together.

"I guess that makes sense," added Angus. "Um, but so what?"

Rex gave up and started walking back toward his house. "The pair of you are idiots," he remarked. "If you want to get results, you might as well do it yourself."

Stakeouts are Boring

With a burst of energy, Rex turned and ran, leaping upward to sail over the fence and into Angus's garden. Angus barked at him, muscle memory demanding he react when another animal invaded his turf. Rex wasn't hanging around though. With two bounds, he crossed Angus's lawn and leapt again, this time clearing the fence separating Angus from Dmitry.

A little taken aback, Dmitry asked, "Ah, what are you up to, Rex?"

Rex's nose was already down and working, snuffling an inch above the grass as he searched for the elusive, but now familiar scent. Finding nothing, he lifted his head to reply to the Great Dane.

"You said the pasty wrapper is here?"

Dmitry raised an eyebrow. "Yeah. It's over there," he nodded his head toward an overgrown clematis that was nothing but woody vines.

Rex spotted it instantly, his nose leading him across the lawn with Dmitry hard on his tail.

"You know," Dmitry grumbled, "it's not that I mind so much, but there is an etiquette to observe, old boy."

Rex sighed. "Yes, Dmitry, I'm in your place and I invited myself. There is a case to solve, so ... my apologies."

"Accepted," Dmitry sat on his haunches, freeing a back leg to scratch at his ear. "What are you proposing?"

"Rex is going to track the scent and find the thief!" yipped Angus excitedly.

"Something like that," murmured Rex. He'd taken a good whiff of the paper bag the pasty came in and was backing up a pace to use his eyes for once. Pinning the bag down with his front right paw, he examined what appeared to be teeth marks.

The bag itself was a basic white paper item roughly nine inches square. There were a few crumbs from the puff pastry left inside and the paper had absorbed some of the grease from the pasty, leaving it with a smell that made Rex want to eat the bag even though he knew it would taste terrible.

"What do you make of this?" he asked Dmitry.

The Great Dane shuffled into position next to Rex and peered down at the bag. It had been chewed through on one side, a gaping hole left where a creature had fought to get to the contents hidden within.

Trying to think analytically, Dmitry said, "Sharp teeth. A predator most likely."

"Or a scavenger," Rex countered, reminding Dmitry of the rubbish bins at Angus's place. "It came in through my kitchen window, so it must be agile. And small."

Rex tilted his head up to look at the trees. He knew it wasn't a squirrel; their scent was hardwired into his brain and the critters knew to stay out of his garden. It was something else and whatever it was, neither he nor the two dogs he was with had ever encountered one before.

"What are we looking at?" asked Angus, popping up between Dmitry's front paws.

Startled, Dmitry jumped back a pace and when he saw who it was, he shot his head around to look at the fence. How had the tiny dog jumped it?

"Oh, that is not going to go down well," the Great Dane commented when he saw the freshly dug hole. "You know they are going to blame me for that, right?"

"Just fill it back in after I go back through," Angus made the solution sound simple. Looking at Rex, he asked, "Right, what's next?"

Rex continued to look at the trees. Was it out there now, watching them? What was it that could scale the side of a house, steal food, and sneak out again, touching so little that it barely even left a scent? Why was there only one of them?

"Rex?" Angus prompted.

His eyes still glued to the trees, Rex said, "We lie in wait."

Rex returned to his own garden, leaping the fences with ease, and Angus burrowed back through the hole he'd made, popping up on the other side to shake the dirt from his coat.

"You uprooted a rose," Dmitry complained. "I'm telling you, they will notice that."

Angus trotted off, utterly unbothered about his neighbour's stupid rose. "Oh, quit whining and find a spot to hide in." He was going to burrow under a viburnum, certain the foliage would hide him from view.

Looking around his garden, Dmitry muttered, "That's easy for you to say." At well over seven feet tall if he stood upright, Dmitry needed a lot of room if he was going to attempt to hide. He tried under the garden bench first, but it fell over before he couldn't get his back under it. The same thing happened when he tried to squeeze under the table and chairs. He trampled a juniper in a bid to get his body beneath its low running horizontal branches, and settled for peering out from behind the shed.

In the time it took the other two to figure out where to go, Rex had dealt with all the essential pre-stakeout tasks. He emptied his bladder and taken a good drink to make sure he stayed hydrated – nothing worse for the brain than running dry. He wanted something to eat and would have gone inside to bug Albert for a biscuit if he didn't already know what the answer was going to be.

Being reminded of his biscuit ban only strengthened his resolve, so when Rex settled into his own hiding spot, in a corner by the back fence where widdle from the local cats using the alley on the other side would disguise his scent, he was relaxed yet on high alert. Ready to pounce, yet using minimal energy, he laid his head on his front paws and accepted he was going to be there for hours.

That was how stakeouts went. There was nothing to do but observe and stay as quiet as possible.

"This is fun," yipped Angus.

"Shhhh," said Rex.

"Huh? What was that?" asked Angus, jumping out from his hiding place to peer through an old knothole in the fence. "I couldn't hear what you said."

"We're supposed to be quiet," hissed Rex. "Whatever this animal is, it won't come if it believes we are waiting for it. Be still, stay quiet, and holler if you see anything that might be our target."

Buzzing with excitement, Angus yipped again, then lowered his voice when he realised what he'd done. "Sorry.

Quiet. Right. I'll, um ... I'll just ... yes." Angus went back to hide under his bush.

Ten minutes went by, and Rex began to feel the tension easing from his shoulders. Perhaps the dogs would manage to stay quiet, and he was worried about nothi ...

"How long do you think this might take?" Dmitry asked.

Rex could feel his top lip curling. Harsh words were gathering in his mouth and requesting permission to assail the ears of his companions.

To cap it off, the back door to Angus's house opened and a voice called out. "Angus! Walkies!"

Angus exploded from his hiding spot. "Walkies!" he echoed, too excited to resist.

Rex bit down on what he had to say, opting instead to listen to what Dmitry might say now that Angus was gone. Was the Great Dane about to announce that stakeouts were boring? Five minutes later, just when Rex was feeling optimistic about Dmitry's involvement, he heard the Great Dane begin to snore.

"Dear Lord," Rex grumped, rising to his feet. There was no chance they were going to catch the critter today. Intending to bark a few insults at Dmitry before he went inside, Rex stepped out of his hiding place and that was when it hit him.

Monkey Badger

The scent of the animal appeared the moment he came away from the smell of cat widdle. It had probably been there for several minutes, but the same overpowering cat stench that hid his scent had stopped Rex's nose from detecting it.

Rex froze, focussing everything on his nose and what it could smell. The scent pulled his head to the right just in time to see something arrive on top of the garden fence. It was the opposite side to Angus, not that it would have made a blind bit of difference because Angus was no longer there.

The creature looked at Rex and Rex looked at it. Kind of like a cat and a badger had an oddly shaped baby, it had bushy grey fur, a banded tail, and appeared to be wearing an old-time bandit's mask.

"What the heck are you?" Rex wanted to know, too stunned by the strange animal to remember that he ought to be attacking it.

"Ha!" chittered the creature. "I'm your worst nightmare!"

Rex frowned. "The one where the vet decides to lighten my trousers even though no one has asked him too? I have that dream all the time and it scares me so much I have to sleep under the couch for the rest of the night."

The creature looked confused for a second. "Okay, so maybe I'm your second worst nightmare." it lifted its left paw, which had until then been hidden behind its back. In it was a chocolate bar; a kid's size one. Sticking it between its teeth the critter then ran along the fence top, jumped into a tree, and ran up it like a squirrel, chittering insults until it was out of sight.

All too late, Rex woke from his reverie, barking and snarling at the base of the oak tree.

Whatever he'd just encountered saw no reason to answer, but a minute later, the wrapper from the chocolate bar drifted down out of the tree to land at Rex's feet.

"Oh, I'm gonna get you, weird little monkey badger. I'm gonna get you good."

A plan was brewing inside his head. It was complex and required help from his unreliable neighbours, but if they could fire their brains up to speed, Rex believed he could catch the thieving monkey badger in the act.

"Rex."

Rex spun about at the sound of his name. His human had the back door open and was putting his wellies on. Rex didn't need a walk. Truthfully, he didn't want one right now, but perhaps he could find something he needed at the park.

Never Work with Animals

Hours later, when the sun had set and Albert was in the living room watching television, Rex gently nudged the kitchen door shut and opened the back door. It took four attempts, the handle on the backdoor not designed for a dog's paw. He found Angus waiting outside, the terrier's tail wagging madly to be part of the plan.

Rex hadn't intended to involve Dmitry; the dog was just too big and gangly to ever be stealthy, but he needed Dmitry to speak to Janice and once the Great Dane knew the plan, there was no way around letting him tag along.

"So you understand your part in this, Janice?" Rex asked after going over his ludicrously simple plan twice.

Janice, her eyes failing to meet in the middle, slowly rotated her head so it was more or less looking in Rex's direction.

She hiccupped, then said, "Huh?"

Am I at a low point? Rex questioned silently in his head. *How far have I sunk if I am willing to call upon a cat to help me?*

Since Rex hadn't answered, the cat and was now

banging his head repeatedly against the front of the washing machine, Angus ran through it again.

"Yeah. Yeah, I remember now," drawled Janice, sounding sleepy. "I'll get into position then, shall I?"

Rex used his sweetest tone. "If you wouldn't mind, Janice."

The cat looked about, swayed a touch to one side, overcorrected, but then leapt to the top of the refrigerator.

Albert left the window open to create a flow of air on all but the coldest days and that had to be where the monkey badger had been getting in. Rex was colourfully descriptive and made sure not to embellish when he explained to the others the creature he'd met. They made suitable sounds of awe, questioning what it could be and where it might have come from.

With no other name for it, 'money badger' was agreed upon without the subject being discussed. They also agreed upon the need to catch it since it was breaking into their homes, an offense no dog would tolerate, and was getting them into trouble, all three dogs having copped the blame for one of the money badger's crimes in the last few days.

Rex went to his hiding place, nudging another door open to reveal a broom cupboard. Heading for a shady spot behind the vacuum cleaner, he almost shot out of his skin when Dmitry yelped in fear.

"What the devil is the matter with you now?" Rex demanded to know. "What do you think will happen to this plan if my human hears you and comes to investigate?"

Dmitry was all the way over on the far side of the kitchen and cowering with his tail between his legs.

"It's the vacuum cleaner!" he squealed, doing his best to keep his voice low. "How can you be so close to it? Aren't you terrified it will go for your tail?"

Rex looked at Angus, checking to see if the giant Great Dane was for real. When he got a shrug, Rex did his best to reason with the enormous hound.

"It's just a machine, Dmitry. Humans use them to clean up mess. I don't know why, so it's no good asking me that. It's literally the dumbest thing they do because the mess is always there again five minutes later. Look though," Rex nudged the plug with his nose. "It's not even plugged in."

"Just keep it away from me," gibbered Dmitry.

Hanging his head for a second and muttering unkind things under his breath, Rex sucked in a deep breath and tried again.

"I'm just going to get the lure, okay? I promise I will try to shut the door and the big scary vacuum cleaner away once I have it. Okay?" Rex checked to see if the Great Dane was going to make a racket, but Dmitry had his eyes tightly shut and wasn't answering.

Rex retrieved what he'd found at the park from behind the vacuum cleaner. Once Albert had let him off the lead, he'd run full pelt for a spot all the dogs knew. Close to the bin, which was generally overflowing, the schoolkids discarded what their parents had packed for their lunch. You had to get there at the right time of the day because the good stuff was always snagged by the first dog to come along. He'd gotten lucky today.

Okay, so what had actually happened was he found a sandwich and picked it up with the intention of bringing it home. Rex convinced himself he could carry it undetected in his mouth, and possibly he could have done precisely that had Albert ruined it.

"What have got there?" Rex's human had asked, triggering an automatic response whereby Rex swallowed the sandwich whole.

Cursing, he then had to find another. The second time he had to race a saucy Rough Collie to the treat because she's smelled it too. Rex knew her well enough from previous visits to the park and was quite keen to get to 'know her better'.

He doubted that was going to happen now though if the insults she hurled at his back were any indication. She'd beaten him to it, and he'd shoulder barged her off the trophy before she could sink her teeth in.

Unfortunately, it was over a foot long, so he stood no chance of hiding it in his mouth and to his great horror he discovered that it was loaded with jalapenos.

"Put that down, Rex," commanded Albert, an order with which Rex was only too happy to comply.

Finally, luck chose to rescue him as they headed out of the park, Rex's nose picked up the scent of a kebab. Ahead of him someone's hastily eaten dinner had spilled, the shrapnel of lettuce and shredded white cabbage hiding the live grenade of juicy meat.

He had to feign a need to pee so Albert would stop, and when the old man wasn't looking, he scooped it into his mouth. Then began a battle of mind over matter as his brain demanded he swallow the wonderful morsels.

"It's still warm," he whimpered, strings of saliva threatening to run from the corners of his mouth.

"Everything all right, old boy?" asked Albert, peering at his dog.

"Yes, yes, everything's fine," Rex lied, questioning whether it was really worth this much torture just to get back his biscuit ration. *'It's not just biscuits,'* he told himself. *'It's principle too!'*

Principle or not, the pieces of kebab were still where he'd left them, in a slightly dusty spot hidden from sight between the mop bucket and the vacuum cleaner, and they stunk to high heaven. At least to the dogs they did.

Rex backed out of the broom cupboard and turned around to find Angus and Dmitry staring at him with pained expressions.

His fear forgotten, Dmitry's paws were carrying him across the kitchen.

"I could smell that when we walked in," he murmured, unable to take his eyes off the pieces of meat hanging from Rex's mouth. "I just figured it was what your human had for dinner."

Angus's jowls quivered with barely contained excitement. "The monkey badger won't need all of that, surely."

"Yeah," intoned Dmitry. "There's easily enough for us each to have a small piece now."

Rex curled his lip. "Back away, both of you. I carried this all the way home in my mouth. If anyone is going to get to eat it, it's me. No one is eating it though because we are going to use it as bait to get the monkey badger to come in. When he smells this, which he will, he'll come through the window, Janice will jump from the fridge to the shelf by the window and swipe the catch to close it. The little thief will be caught red-handed, my human will hear us barking and come running to find the culprit right on the kitchen counter where his pasty was earlier today. Case closed, job well done, double biscuit ration for Rex."

Dmitry and Angus didn't like it, but they deferred to Rex – it was his plan after all, and they were curious to see the monkey badger critter for themselves. They each found hiding places, backing into dark corners of the kitchen.

Angus hid in a cubby hole where the tea towels hung. It placed him directly beneath the meat, but that was okay because he was too short to reach it. Rex reversed into the broom cupboard once more, making sure the door was halfway closed for the shadow it cast across him. On the other side of the kitchen, Dmitry lowered himself to the tile where the moonlight coming through the window couldn't reach.

They were hidden.

But they were not exactly silent.

"Dmitry, I can hear you drooling," Rex hissed from his hiding place.

The Great Dane's whisper came back, "I can't help it. The meat smells soooo good."

"For goodness sake, get a grip of yourself. If we catch the monkey badger critter, there will be biscuits for everyone, and I promise to forego my share of the meat so you and Angus can share it."

"Equal shares," piped up Angus instantly.

"Hey, why equal shares," challenged Dmitry. "I'm twenty times your size. We should share it in proportion to our body weight."

Angus had something rude to say in reply and Rex had to get in quick before anyone saw fit to start barking.

"Just shut up the pair of you! Stay quiet for a few minutes and the critter might actually appear. Do you think you pair of dopey mongrels can manage that?"

Rex got a snippy response from both Angus and Dmitry, who might never agree about how to share the meat but were on the same page about their pedigree status.

Silence returned.

For a while. It was replaced less than a minute later by the sound of escaping gas.

"Did you just fart, Dmitry?" Rex demanded to know.

Automatically, Dmitry lied, "No."

Rex was about to call the Great Dane on his response

when a sound coming from the direction of the open window stole the words from his mouth.

A shadow flitted through the moonlight, enormous against the back wall of the kitchen. Poised, the muscles in his back legs bunched and ready to leap, Rex crouched like a coiled spring in the broom cupboard.

Something paused on the edge of the window. It was hard for Rex to see from his angle and moving would give himself away, so he held his breath, convinced one of the dogs was about to say or do something that would alert the monkey badger and send it running.

And that's precisely what happened.

Sort of.

Mayhem

Dmitry heard the critter's claws on the edge of the shelf by the window when it took a first tentative step inside and misread them as Angus making his move to get the meat.

Exploding from his hiding place, the Great Dane threw himself at the kitchen counter to get there first. Unfortunately, he forgot that linoleum has a low coefficient of friction, and his gangly legs went out from under him before he could get moving.

Startled by Dmitry's sudden movement, Angus jumped half out of his skin – he'd been staring in rapt horror at the enormous bear-sized shadow the monkey badger was casting on the far wall. Jolted into moving, he was running out of his cubby hole when Dmitry crashed to the floor, the Great Dane's face landing next to his.

Rex yelled, "Janice now!" expecting the cat to leap into action as planned. All she had to do was swipe at the bar holding the window open – something she assured them she could do – and the thieving critter would be trapped inside the house.

What Rex got in response was a snore. The bedlam that was Dmitry racing to get to the bait demanded Rex bolt from the broom cupboard. He could see something on the shelf by the window, but before he could get a good look at it, Angus ran right through his front paws.

Trying to get away from what he assumed was the bear whose shadow he'd seen, Angus fled just as Dmitry crashed to the floor. Looking over his shoulder and thus not where he was going, he used Rex's legs like a cat flap.

Both dogs howled and barked as they went crashing to the floor.

Frantic to get to the meat before anyone else could, Dmitry jumped up to get his paws under his body. Rex saw him, knew what he was doing, and launched himself to intercept.

"You're going to scare the monkey badger away!" he raged, ramming Dmitry's ribs in the dark.

The Great Dane, his almost two-hundred-pound bulk shunted sideways, lost control and slammed into the refrigerator. With the addition of Rex's weight and inertia, the appliance chose to obey basic physical laws and started to topple.

Asleep on top of it, Janice-the-stoner cat's eyes opened – something was very wrong with the planet. It was tilting to one side, and she didn't like it. She didn't like it at all.

Angus, having skidded to a halt near the kitchen door, had turned around to discover there was no bear chasing him. What he could see was Dmitry and Rex smashing into the fridge and … something high above them coming down from the shelf by the kitchen window. The silhouette was small – smaller than Angus anyway and it was heading directly for the meat.

Seizing his chance, Angus's tiny canine brain calculated angles, moving trajectories, and required velocity. Then, accepting that the maths was far too complex, he threw caution to the wind and started running anyway.

High above the dogs, Janice was now fully alert and digging into the top of the refrigerator with her claws. The problem with that was how ineffective her claws were proving to be and that the angle of the surface on which she sat continued to increase.

Abandoning the idea that she might be able to stay where she was, Janice scrambled to get to safety.

Angus bounded across the kitchen, jumped onto Rex's thigh as he fell into Dmitry, ran a pace then leapt onto Dmitry's back. Digging in with his claws to gain traction, the West Highland Terrier ran up the Great Dane even as all three dogs fell though the gap the refrigerator once occupied. At the apex of his climb, Angus leapt, folding his paws backward for optimum aerodynamics.

The only thing that mattered was the meat. His aim was true. He was going to be able to get his teeth on the succulent kebab strips before gravity pulled him back down.

Janice landed on his face.

The fridge hit the wall, blocking the back door, and sending an array of magnets raining to the floor. Notes and postcards they had held in place fluttered down like confetti as Dmitry, Rex, Angus, and Janice landed one atop the other in that order.

The door from the living room burst open, Albert racing to see if there really was a rhinoceros having sex with a walrus in his kitchen sink – that's what it had sounded like.

"What the heck is ..." Albert flicked the light switch by the door, illuminating the mayhem of his kitchen.

The dogs all looked his way, freezing and wondering if they should just smile and pretend they were having a bit of boisterous fun. Sitting on top of the pile, Janice chose to lick a paw and make like nothing was happening.

Albert wasn't really looking at the pets though, his attention was on the racoon eating a piece of kebab meat on his kitchen countertop.

"A racoon," he blurted, unable to believe his eyes.

As if given leave by Albert's remark, the racoon picked up the last piece of meat, scaled the net curtain, and went out the window.

For a second, no one moved or said anything. Until a Sunday ham Albert had bought ready for his family visiting chose to shift inside the fridge. It hit the door, knocking it open whereupon it and most of the rest of the contents chose to vomit all over the assembled pets.

"Ooooh, ham," yipped Angus.

An hour later, Rex was finally invited back inside the house. He was cold, wet, and somewhat miserable having been cleaned off with the garden hose. Albert had wielded it mercilessly, blasting the yoghurt slime, sticky jam, and vinegary pickled onion juice from Rex's coat while berating him continuously.

The neighbours had come, collecting Angus, Dmitry, and Janice to be taken home for their own ablutions and it was in that doorstep conversation that Albert discovered where the racoon had come from. Not native to England or even Europe, the creature was a pet owned by Mrs Lee at number fourteen. It had been missing for days.

Albert explained all this to Rex as he scrubbed soap into his fur coat. Rex, suffering his bath in silence. With his ears down and his expression somewhere south of grumpy, he was about as disappointed with how things ended as a dog could be.

However, the final straw came when Albert commented, "I have to wonder, Rex, if the racoon got the idea to steal food from copying you."

Vet's Waiting Room

Vet's Waiting Room

Rex huffed and tried to get comfortable. The wipe-clean linoleum floor might be a practical surface for the waiting room at a veterinary surgery, but it possessed far too little friction. Anything other than lying down meant one's paws slowly slid outwards.

Keeping them in place demanded rigid muscle control which became tiring before very long. Perhaps that was the point, Rex mused. If the pets couldn't stand, they were far less likely to run away. Also, their humans were better able to manoeuvre them into the vet's room if they couldn't get a decent purchase on the floor.

It was a conspiracy and no mistake.

With a meaningful harrumph, Rex laid his head on his paws. He didn't want to see the vet. Yes, he had a cut to his mouth that was bothering him and a slightly loose tooth, but he felt certain it would take care of itself if left alone.

His human, however, had insisted they needed to get him checked out.

Huffing and making sure he did so loud enough that his

human could hear, Rex grumped and wished he was feeling gassy. Letting one go underneath the old man's chair was the least he could do for the indignity to follow.

"It's the smell," complained a Basset Hound to Rex's left. "All vet's waiting rooms smell the same: Chemically clean."

"And fear," added a nervous sounding Golden Retriever. "They always smell like fear," he gibbered before wetting the floor in terror. "Wahhh!" He leapt to his feet. "I'm incontinent! I wasn't before I came in here!" he ran for the door, his claws scrabbling for purchase and finding almost none on the friction-free linoleum.

Reaching the end of his lead, the human it was attached to snarled something unrepeatable and yanked in the other direction.

The Labrador's feet went out and he crashed to earth.

One of the surgery doors opened to reveal a small woman with ginger hair and glasses. Leaning out, she called, "Mrs Cane with Trevor?"

"Oh, no!" cried the Labrador. "That's me. Play dead. Play dead." Trevor let his tongue loll from his mouth and stiffened all his muscles.

Mrs Cane was on her feet and tutting.

"Really, Trevor? Every time? Every time we come here you pull this stunt and every time it ends the same."

Trevor didn't move.

Mrs Cane unzipped a pouch on her hip, the slow and deliberate noise from it causing Trevor's eyes to twitch.

Around the waiting room, six dogs of various shapes and sizes sat up and paid attention – they all knew what was in the pouch.

Leaning over, Trevor's owner wafted the gravy bone under his nose and gave the lead a tug.

"Still dead, huh?"

She straightened back to upright, opened her hand and dropped the biscuit treat directly above her dog's muzzle.

Unable to resist, though he hated himself for it, Trevor bounced onto his feet just in time to see his human catch the gravy bone in her other hand and flick it in the direction of the vet's open door.

With his tongue flapping from the right side of his mouth, Trevor raced after it, his lead dropping from Mrs Cane's hand when she let it go and waltzed casually after him.

The biscuit slid over the threshold of the surgery, closely followed by Trevor who had suddenly realised what was happening and had dumped his backside on the floor in a bid to prevent the inevitable.

With a yelp, he went sideways through the door, closely followed by Mrs Cane who shut it behind her. The last thing the dogs in the waiting room heard was the crunch of the biscuit.

Silence reigned for several seconds.

"So what are you in for?" asked the Basset Hound, striking up a conversation with Rex.

Rex had no interest in talking to anyone, but he didn't feel a need to be rude just because he was feeling grumpy about his situation.

"Took a knock to the head leaping onto a moving power boat. I have a loose tooth. You?"

The Basset Hound looked like he was about to say something, but paused, a worried look creeping across his face. He began panting and looking around for a water bowl.

"You okay?" Rex wondered if he ought to move away.

"I, ah, I ate a cake mix. Apparently, its one where you

just need to add water and the raising agents are already in it. They left it on the floor, how was I supposed to know I wasn't supposed to eat it?"

"Was it in a shopping bag?" asked a cat, leering out from her carry cage on the seat opposite. Her tone was mocking as befitted a cat.

The Basset didn't answer, but held his breath and strained.

Basically, Rex figured, the dog was baking a cake inside his stomach. It was rising and expanding and one way or another it was going to make a bid for freedom shortly.

Another surgery door opened.

"Is there a Fred out here?" asked a male vet. He was tall and skinny. So tall, in fact, and so skinny, he looked a lot like a bleached, shaved cactus. His polo shirt reached his trousers, but only just.

The Basset Hound took off like a rocket, running for the surgery door and dragging his human like a kid with a kite.

Less than two seconds after the door closed, a sound like a … like a … oh, there's just no parallel that is any better than just describing it.

Let's just say Fred's human and the vet cried out in horror and when it was done Fred felt a whole lot better. Also, it might not have been chocolate cake going in, but it sure looked like it coming out.

"Dogs," remarked the cat. "So disgusting."

Rex lifted an eyebrow. "Oh? And what are you in for, furball?"

The cat had been inspecting a front paw, its focus solely on its own digits. Now flicking its gaze at Rex, the cat, a silky looking Burmese, flashed out five razor sharp claws like a character from a horror movie.

"Just a check-up, fleabag."

"I hate cats," growled a Boxer. "Always acting so superior."

"It's not an act, mongrel," the cat's voice echoed out from within its carry cage.

Rex put his head down and tried to shut out the voices.

He dozed for a few moments, his slumber interrupted in a brutal manner when he heard his own name being called.

Goodness, he hated trips to the vet.

More by Steve Higgs

vinci-books.com/paranormal-nonsense

Fight a demon, investigate a werewolf biker gang, have tea with mum ...

When a master vampire starts killing people in his hometown, private investigator Tempest Michaels takes it personally. He doesn't believe in the paranormal, but when a third victim turns up with bite marks in her lifeless throat, can he really dismiss the possibility that the monster is real?

Turn the page for a free preview…

Paranormal Nonsense: Chapter One

THE WRONG ROUTE HOME

Wednesday, 22nd September 2316hrs

She didn't see the man until she was quite close to him. Her focus was instead on the phone under her nose as she typed a scolding text message to her friend, Sarah. She had regretfully agreed to a double date so Sarah's boyfriend's pal, Darren, would have someone to talk to. Sarah claimed that Darren was really good-looking and athletic, which turned out to be true, but he was also an utter bore who talked only about himself. Walking home in the dark and angry about her crappy evening, she was texting Sarah to tick her off for abandoning her so she could sneak off to suck face with Chris. Darren hadn't even offered to buy her a drink, so with her purse now deflated, she was walking home unable to afford a taxi.

It was only when she pressed send on the message and looked up, that she saw the man on the dark path ahead of her. Instantly feeling anxious, she wished now that she had taken the longer route along the main road and not the shorter one by the river. The river path was much faster, but it was also dark because half the lampposts had long since stopped working.

The man wasn't moving, and her feet had come to an involuntary stop, so they now faced each other on the path with about ten yards between them. He looked to be wearing a dark suit. The little bit of light coming between the trees was catching on the shine of his shoes and the white vee of the shirt either side of his dark tie. He still hadn't moved but there was nothing threatening about his stance, and she could see both his hands; they hung empty and loose at his sides. His face was hidden in shadow, but what she could see, from his shoulder to waist proportion, told her he was seriously muscular.

Feeling silly when she realised she was just standing still and becoming ever more aware of the cool September air on her exposed skin, she called out to him. "Hello?"

In response, he raised his head. Slowly and deliberately, he brought his eyes up to meet hers. In the darkness of the shadows, she hadn't realised he'd been looking down. He leaned forward just a little, moving his face into a thin shaft of light coming through the trees.

Then he smiled at her.

There was nothing pleasant or engaging about the smile. The man's smile implied bad things were about to happen and when he opened his lips, the smile showed far too many teeth and canines that were distinctly longer than they ought to be.

A heartbeat passed as they stared at each other, but then he moved, exploding into action toward her. Too shocked to scream, she spun away. Her feet slipped on the debris and mud of the path, causing her to pitch forward. Almost falling, she corrected her motion with a hand on the ground and took off at a sprint back in the direction of the pub.

Naturally athletic, having been a sprinter through her school years, she hit full speed after a few yards. With the passage of air whipping her hair around, she felt confident she could outpace the man. The pub would soon be in sight; a faint glow from the outside lights already visible through the trees. There would be safety there, so as her breath started to tug in her chest, she pushed harder, determined to get away from whatever menace the man intended.

The blow to her head came as a surprise. She had no sense that he was even close to her, but it landed hard behind her right ear, instantly knocking her off balance and stunning her at the same time. She stumbled, legs tangling as the sideways shunt ruined her forward motion.

As the barely visible concrete beneath her feet became a painful eventuality, she put her hands out to arrest the impact. Out of control, she hit first with her right hip and, still spinning, crashed over onto her back. Her left shoulder bit painfully into the rough path, tearing her skin and the back of her head smacked into the unyielding ground. She tasted blood. Coming to rest in the nettles and litter at the side of the path, she lifted her legs to fend off his attack.

He wasn't attacking, though. Instead, he stood calmly next to her feet. Involuntarily, she made a little choking sound of fright and glanced around for help, even though she already knew none was coming.

The man's suit looked unruffled, and his expression was calm, serene almost, as if nothing untoward was occurring and he perhaps wanted to ask her the time.

Confused, though still terrified, she propped herself up on her elbows and squirmed back a few feet to get some distance between them. The move rewarded her with fresh stings on the exposed skin of her shoulders as she backed into yet more nettles. The pain barely registered.

"What do you want?" she demanded, her voice wobbling with adrenaline.

She regretted the question instantly for it prompted the man to crouch. He didn't touch her but came as close as he could without doing so. Leaning forward, he brought his face within inches of hers.

"I want to drink your blood, little lamb," he said, his voice calm and almost soothing with a faint European accent.

Then he hit her.

As she reeled from the blow, a massive hand seized her hair and twisted her head cruelly to one side. She grabbed at his hands, but it made no difference; the fist continued to twist around until it pushed her face into the dirt. She scrambled with her legs, trying to find purchase so she could fight him off, but she was no match for his strength or superior body weight. His knee went into the small of her back and she could no more move a building than shake him off.

She felt him move closer yet, bending right over her to nuzzle her neck like a lover might, and then he bit down into her soft flesh. Hot liquid ran over her skin, and she knew it was her blood. It began to pool under her chin and was getting in her hair. She wanted to fight back but all too soon she found that doing so felt like a lot of effort.

The man held her in place as her frantic struggles lessened. Blearily, she could see something silvery. He had moved again, fiddling in a pocket to produce a small jug. And he was doing something with it now, touching it to her skin where he had bitten her. She tried to focus, but she was getting a headache from her hammering pulse and the jug didn't seem all that important. Her heart felt like it was banging in her chest and her eyes wanted to close. Wondering why her eyes were so heavy was her final thought as unconsciousness took her.

In the moonlight, the man stood back to watch her final breaths, the silver chalice held carefully in his left hand. Its contents threatened to spill over, so as he set off back down the path, he cradled it with both hands and was soon swallowed by the dark.

Paranormal Nonsense: Chapter Two

THE BODY OF VICTORIA TURNBULL

Thursday, 23rd September 0500hrs

PC Amanda Harper checked her watch: 0513hrs. It was neither light nor dark. The first rays of sun had begun to pierce the gloom yet hadn't really done anything to lighten the surroundings. She was standing on a narrow path that bordered the river Medway near to Maidstone. The path was tranquil, picturesque, and thoroughly safe during daylight hours. She had walked along it many times. But in the dark it was far less pleasant. Starkly, she found it foreboding and anxiety-inducing and was telling herself to stop imagining the things rustling in the undergrowth were coming to get her.

Her shift had started at 1800hrs the previous evening, and she should be finishing work in less than an hour. Experience had taught her that it was not going to go like that, though. After seven years on the beat, this was not her first murder scene and there was no way they were going to replace her this side of breakfast. If anything, they needed more people on the scene to manage human traffic, keep crowds back, and assist the forensic team to conduct their investigation. She would be swept up into the day of important tasks that needed doing fast.

She checked her watch again and shifted her feet a little. Trying not to look like she was dancing, she moved her arms about a bit to keep the stiffness out and the cold away. The warmth of August was long forgotten, replaced by the coolness of autumn. It was dry at least, but the early morning mist from the river was damp, and the cool air had penetrated the layers of her uniform more than half an hour ago.

Sgt Dave Barnet appeared out of the gloom a few yards away from where he had undoubtedly been involved in something far more interesting than perimeter security. Dave fancied her. She knew it, although he had never said anything and was quite polite and avoided flirting in general. She could tell though when she caught him glancing away when she turned, when he smiled at her and gave one too many work-related compliments.

She was attractive. Amanda accepted that as one accepts that their hair is brown, or their eyes are blue. She understood that genetics had given her a curvaceous figure, high cheekbones, flowing hair and a strong jawline that could have led to modelling. It was never a career choice that interested her, although right now the thought of a bikini shoot in the Bahamas for some new swimwear firm sounded like a vast improvement. Come to think of it, topless glamour modelling sounded good when compared to freezing her nipples off next to a river in the early hours of the morning.

Dave looked over, caught her eye and began walking towards her. Emerging from the gloom, his face was grim.

"What have we got?" she asked.

"Nasty and weird murder, that's what," he answered. "Another bitten throat. Poor girl would have bled to death, and it was clearly quite violent." Neither said anything for a moment while the river mist swirled about them.

"Is it like the others? Same MO?"

"I wouldn't go on record with that, but yes, essentially it appears to be the same." Even up close it was difficult to see his features in the dark, but he sounded weary and stressed.

Amanda had seen a few bodies. Murder in Kent was relatively rare, but she had been around long enough to have attended a fair number of murder scenes. The recent series, if they could call it that, was something else though. Each of the three victims, assuming this was number three, had been alone when attacked at night and were found with a wound to their throat. The press had gotten hold of it almost two weeks ago after the second murder and were already calling it 'the vampire attacks', or other such crude but catchy names. The term *The Vampire* had been coined immediately by *The Weald Word*, a local paper more used to reporting jumble sale successes and prize-winning turnips. Their lead reporter led with the legend: 'Vampire killer loose in Maidstone.' It was published the morning following the second murder. The national press seized upon it in what was a slow news week, and now it was hard to think of the perpetrator by another term.

Amanda squinted at her Sergeant's face, trying to get a read of his expression in the gloom. "So, what is the scene like? Likelihood of usable evidence?"

"Just like the last two, I think. Not much of anything to help us," he replied, his tone carrying little inflection. "There will be saliva around the wound, but that has already been checked and led us nowhere. Other than that, this guy doesn't leave anything we can use. The SOCO chaps will be thorough, but whether they are able to find anything helpful …" He stopped speaking when his radio squawked, the sound cutting through the quiet stillness of the dawn in a shocking burst of noise. The call was for him, so he left her there with a brief nod as he went.

Another forty-five minutes passed as the sun struggled lazily upwards. It lit the sky, making it feel like morning by the time PC Brad Hardacre emerged from the trees surrounding the white tents of the crime scene. She spotted him because she was looking the wrong way again, thoroughly bored with watching the ducks sleep on the bank next to her. Just before 0600hrs, she had actually performed her function and turned away two joggers as they ran down the path towards her, presumably on their usual route. Other than that, she had done nothing for the last two hours.

She checked her watch: 0602hrs.

"Good morning, Amanda, how has your day been so far?" hallooed Brad with enthusiasm as he approached. Brad was an okay guy - most of them were with the odd exception - but she quite liked him and might have been interested if they didn't work together.

"It has been sucky mostly, Brad, but nowhere near as bad as the victim had it." She gestured with her head to the tents.

"Another vampire victim?" Brad asked while making his canines stick out below his top lip.

"Didn't you check in with control when you arrived?" she asked with exasperation, "You know the protocols, Brad. How can you know what is happening if you avoid getting a brief?"

He smiled and waggled his eyebrows conspiratorially. "I

quite like the idea of a vampire in Maidstone. It adds a bit of badly needed coolness to the dreary landscape. Vampires are cool, right? Besides, the Chief can eat my pants."

"If you are a teenage girl and a virgin and have watched *Twilight* too many times then maybe vampires are cool. Otherwise, they are for geeks with *Buffy the Vampire Slayer* fantasies." She looked him dead in the face, "I doubt the victim will agree that vampires are cool." She was being a little hard on him - a little banter around horrible events is completely normal, but he needed to reel it in for his own good.

"Well, now that you are here, you can stand watch on this lonely, boring path while I get warm, get some blood back into my limbs, and get a cup of tea. I'm off to see what is going on." With that, she headed toward the tents.

Grab your copy...
vinci-books.com/paranormal-nonsense

About the Author

When Steve Higgs wrote his debut novel, *Paranormal Nonsense*, he was a captain in the British Army. He would like to pretend that he had one of those careers that must be blacked out and generally denied by the government, and that he has to change his name and move constantly because he is still on the watch list in several countries. In truth, though, he started out as a mechanic - not like Jason Statham in the film by that name, sneaking around as a hitman, but more like one of those sleazy guys who charges a fortune and keeps your car for a week even though the only thing you went in for was a squeaky door hinge.

At school, he was largely disinterested in all subjects except creative writing, for which he won his first prize at the age of ten. However, calling it the first prize he won suggests that there were other prizes, which is not the case. Awards may yet come, but in the meantime, he enjoys writing mystery and thriller novels and claims to have more than a hundred books forming a restless queue in his mind because they are desperate to be written.

Now retired from the military, he lives in southeast England with a duo of lazy sausage dogs. Surrounded by rolling hills, brooding castles, and vineyards, he doubts he'll ever leave, the beer is just too good.

www.ingramcontent.com/pod-product-compliance
Ingram Content Group UK Ltd.
Pitfield, Milton Keynes, MK11 3LW, UK
UKHW040923100426
469759UK00003B/35